She could still feel the brush of Matt's lips against hers as he whispered. "I think I'm falling in love with you."

At that moment, caught up in the spell of romance cast over her moon-drenched veranda, Suzanne was ready, willing to make a commitment to the gentle, young preacher. Her heart pounding, she leaned her head against Matt's chest and closed her eyes.

"Not now, not now," the cadence of her heart seemed to warn.

"Not now, not now," the rhythm repeated until, regretfully, Suzanne let the moment slip past.

ARLENE COOK has been gifted with a talent for sharing her faith through the written word. In addition, she is a busy wife, mother, grandmother, and a fulltime office manager for an oil company in Escondido, California.

Forever Yours

Arlene Cook

HARVEST HOUSE PUBLISHERS
Eugene, Oregon 97402

FOREVER YOURS

Dedicated to
William F. Rector, III

Chapter One

"Listen to that wind howl!" Suzanne exclaimed.

She dropped her red pencil on the stack of uncorrected essays on her desk and pulled her Nordic-patterned wool sweater closer around her. Still shivering, the 24-year-old teacher reached up and unclasped the hand-painted barrettes that held her long, chestnut-colored hair back from her heart-shaped face. The thick tresses fell in wavy cascades to her shoulders, forming a lustrous frame for her soft, creamy-white complexion.

Ned Woloski stopped dusting the library shelves in the empty classroom. "It's true," he nodded, "it's as fierce a wind as I've heard in my 70 years in this High Sierra country. We'll have a thick blanket of snow by morning, which is fitting for Thanksgiving Day."

Then suddenly the craggy-faced janitor straightened up, cocked his head, and listened intently. He scowled deeply.

"What is it?" Suzanne questioned nervously.

Without answering, Ned limped hurriedly across the shiny hardwood floor that still smelled as enticingly of fresh varnish as on the first day of school. He reached the row of cathedral windows along the north wall of the 100-year-old classroom that now housed the eighth-grade students. Ned squinted, his eyes scanning the blackness of the sky above.

"Turn off the lights!" he ordered brusquely. "I can't see a thing out there."

Suzanne quickly reached over and flipped the panel of switches on the wall next to her desk. The electrical circuitry was the school's only concession to modernization. Although it was only 6 P.M. the room was thrown into total darkness. Even the glowing embers in the potbellied stove in the far corner failed to cast a flickering shadow on the south wall. A sudden chill raced up her spine—the same chill that had drenched her body one night long ago when, as an unsuspecting 13-year-old, she had been brutally forced into a dark room by a man—a man she. . .

"Ned?"

"Be still!" his voice commanded from across the room.

Suzanne's moment of panic fled, comforted by the assurance of Ned's presence. *Ned is the kindest man I know. He went out of his way to make me feel comfortable when I arrived a year ago in Hastings as a new teacher. He and his wife, Bessie, were the first in this close-knit community to open their home to me.* She felt the muscles in her jaw tighten as she scolded herself, *Will I ever outgrow my childish fear. . .*

"There it is again! Hear it, Miss Flynn? That isn't all nature battling out there." Suzanne strained to hear what was clearly upsetting Ned's gentle nature.

"Hear that noise?" Ned's whisper carried across the room. "It sounds like an airplane in trouble. It's a single-engine craft and it's flying too low!"

"What's he doing out in this storm?" Suzanne asked incredulously.

Now concentrating, she could hear the guttural rumble with its accompanying high-pitched whine as it cried out helplessly above the fury of the season's first heavy onslaught.

"I'm sure he's lost."

"What can we do?" Suzanne asked in a concerned tone as she wove her way cautiously between desks to the other side of the darkened room. Perhaps if she could spot the troubled plane...

"It's gone again," Ned sighed. "All we can do is pray. Hopefully, the lights of Hastings gave the pilot the bearings he needed to find his way out of the storm or at least to the airstrip on the edge of town. In daylight, the old Stevens Ranch has the best strip in the area for emergency landings." Ned sighed and added sadly, "He'll never find it this time of night."

Suzanne was quiet for a moment as she put wings to Ned's prayer and sent it heavenward. Then, retracing her steps across the room to turn on the lights, she added as an afterthought, "You promised to tell me the story of the pioneer Stevens family sometime."

"Sometime isn't now. I've got work to finish," Ned responded, grabbing his oil-coated mop and heading it down the aisle between two rows of desks.

Suzanne sat down at her own desk. She lowered her azure-blue eyes and pretended to read the top essay as she thought.

That's the second time Ned's side-stepped questions on the Stevens' role in Hastings' history. He's spun so many yarns for me during the past year—why does he skirt around one of the area's most prominent early families? Well, whatever the secret, it will never concern me!

They worked in silence, each absorbed in

his own task. Yet, Suzanne knew that both of them were listening fearfully for the returning sound of the endangered airplane. It was impossible for her to know anyone in the plane. Still, the thought of anyone lost out there in the darkness weighed heavily on her heart.

Fifteen minutes passed. The icy wind howled and screeched fair warning of the snowy burden it carried as it rushed mercilessly down the slick granite slopes of the towering Sierra Nevadas and pounced full gale upon the tiny community nestled in a ravine among aspen and pines at the 6000-foot level.

The town was rooted near the headwaters of the Tuolumne River, the same river that gave up millions of dollars in gold to the early '49ers who panned her all the way down to the heart of California's Mother Lode country.

Finally, Ned spoke. Suzanne could tell by the relief in his voice that he counted the pilot safely out of the area and out of harm's reach.

"I can tell you where every kid sits in this room. I know where his parents sat, too. And for some, I can point out where his grandma and grandpa sat, 'cause I was sitting alongside that generation as we studied in this very room together. Rufus Stevens was the first teacher, principal, and janitor—all at the same time. Back then, all the grades were in this one room."

Rufus Stevens? Any relation to the Stevens Ranch? Suzanne wondered silently.

"You're going to miss this world of children when you retire next month, Ned, just as we'll miss you—teachers, students, and parents."

"You're right, mostly. The kids are likely the reason I held off retiring. It was my arthritis that hollered uncle." Then his voice tensed. "There's one somebody I won't miss seeing everyday. My only regret is that she's holding out longer than I am."

Suzanne looked up, startled. "Ned, you're kidding! You've never had an unkind thought about anyone."

"Martha Pettijohn isn't anyone. She's as ornery as a rattlesnake on a hot summer's day."

Suzanne smiled, hoping to lighten the intensity of Ned's statement, if not his mood. "Anyone who teaches third grade is bound to lash out once in awhile. It's called venting frustration. Widow Pettijohn's only snapped at me a couple of times."

Ned stopped sweeping, bent down, scooped up a sheet of paper off the floor, and set it on the desk beside him. Smoothing it out, he mumbled, "It's not like Holly to let her papers fly about."

The distraction over, Ned picked up his dust cloth and the thread of their conversation. "You don't know all there is to know about that serpent-tongued old woman. It would take from now until Christmas Eve to relate the damage she's caused in the past. Fortunately, I remember the year she decided henceforth to call herself "Widow" Pettijohn. So, a couple of years ago we had a few words on the subject. What she thinks I know about her past will keep her quiet until I retire."

Suzanne glanced at her watch. "I don't know about that, but I do know it's time for me to pack up my knapsack and brave the storm. I was due at the parsonage 10 minutes ago."

Ned chuckled. "So the romance with the young minister grows warmer, does it? About time, I'd say. He's been courting you since the day you arrived in town little over a year ago. In fact. . ." He paused undecidedly.

Suzanne felt a blush creep into her cheeks. She turned toward the blackboard and busied herself straightening the chalk tray as she secretly recalled last evening's tender good night. She could still feel the brush of Matt's lips against hers as he whispered, "I think I'm falling in love with you."

At that moment, caught up in the spell of romance cast over her moon-drenched veranda, Suzanne was ready, willing to make a commitment to the gentle, young preacher. Her heart pounding, she leaned her head against Matt's chest and closed her eyes. "Not now, not now," the cadence of her heart seemed to warn. "Not now, not now," the rhythm repeated until, regretfully, Suzanne let the moment slip past.

Without turning from the chalkboard, Suzanne returned to the moment and picked up Ned's cue. "In fact what, Mr. Woloski?"

"Fact is, some of the ladies in the Guild had you two paired up the day the school board announced you'd been hired. The chairman of the board wasted no time in showing the Pastor Matthew Owens your picture."

Suzanne spun around to meet Ned's curious eyes with her own. "The truth is Matt Owens invited me to the parsonage for hot chili and cornbread before the final committee meeting on the Harvest of Blessings we're sponsoring this weekend at the church." She winked and smiled, "Sorry to disappoint the good people of Hastings but the Pastor and I are just good friends."

"We'll see," Ned replied, putting away his cleaning supplies in the storage closet. He washed his hands at the sink at the back of the room, then said, "Get your things together, Miss Flynn. I'm walking you across the square to the parsonage." He held up his hand to stave off an expected protest before adding, "It's not out of my way. I'm going home for a bite of supper myself."

"Thanks, Ned. I don't know why this storm has me spooked. Maybe it's because it's the first one of the season."

Ned grinned. "Maybe you're still a city girl at heart."

"Not me," Suzanne responded strongly. "I love it here. I don't ever want to go back to the world of sirens, street signals, and neon signs."

While putting on her "moon boots," Suzanne asked, "Would you please stick that paper in Holly's desk on the way by? It's bound to fly off again as soon as we open the door."

She was zipping up her boot-length coat when she heard Ned remark, "What's Holly's lunch sack doing in here? Whatever's in it will go bad over this long holiday weekend. I'd better toss it."

"Look inside first," Suzanne suggested. "You know how many dental retainers have been thrown out in students' lunch sacks?"

"I can only guess. I've dug through that dump out back plenty of times over the years while some kid stands by crying and his mother paces back and forth . . ."

Suzanne waited for Ned to continue. When he didn't she glanced his way. He was staring into the sack. "Change your mind about going home for supper?" she teased.

"Better come here, Miss Flynn. The lettuce in this lunch sack isn't exactly the edible kind."

Suzanne hurried to Ned's side and took the brown bag from his extended hand. She looked inside, then up at Ned questioningly.

"How...how much money do you think is in there?" she asked, wide-eyed.

"I have no idea, but I think we'd better count it, then lock it away for the weekend," Ned replied, dumping the contents of the bag onto the nearest desk top.

They counted the money together. "Three hundred and twenty-two dollars is a lot of money for an eighth-grader to accumulate by any means," Ned said.

"It could be her life's savings," Suzanne stated defensively.

"Then why isn't it in the bank? The last place it belongs is in her desk at school."

"I agree," said Suzanne, gathering the money and replacing it in the bag. "It doesn't seem likely that a straight-A student would fail a course in common sense. There must be an acceptable explanation."

"Maybe it's a bank deposit she was supposed to make for her parents' motel," Mr. Woloski offered sincerely. "It could be that they were too busy today, getting ready for holiday tourists, to come in from the main highway themselves. Unfortunately, the bank's closed now until Monday."

Suzanne squeezed Ned's hand and smiled. "You're wonderful. Of course that's what happened. I feel much better now."

"The next question is, what do we do with the money? Holly will get into trouble for leaving it here."

"She'll be in more trouble if the McArthurs don't get the cash back in their possession as soon as possible. I'll take it to the meeting with me tonight. Holly's parents are new members of the committee. I'm sure at least one of them will be there."

"Then let's get you to the church, even if it isn't on time." Ned chuckled at his own humor as he pulled his red wool, tassled cap over his large, protruding ears.

A minute later they were out the door. Ned took a firm grip on the arm of his slim-figured, five-foot-two companion as they braced themselves against the sting of the blinding blizzard. They bent into the wind and trudged through the snow toward the parsonage across the park.

While it took all her physical concentration to keep from slipping and falling, the dedicated teacher could not release Holly McArthur from her mind.

Something's going on with Holly. I should have seen it before this. Last week she fell asleep while I was reading to the class. And Ned was right. It's not like Holly to lose track of her work. What could trouble her so that she would forget and leave $322 in her desk?

Suddenly Ned pulled her up short. They stood together, silently, in the pitch black night, the raging storm swirling around them —listening. From somewhere not far above them came the chilling sound of the single-engine plane still searching frantically, fruitlessly, for a safe harbor.

Suzanne felt a warm tear slip down her cheek. The uneasiness she felt earlier weighed more heavily than ever. Suddenly, she sensed deep within that she and the helpless plane above were united in some mysterious way.

A second tear followed the first.

Chapter Two

"Have some more cornbread while it's still hot," suggested Matt, holding the covered basket toward Suzanne.

"Thanks, I will," she smiled.

Matt pulled back the red-checkered napkin and Suzanne reached for a slice of the moist, steaming homemade cornbread that was Matt's cooking specialty.

His fingers touched hers. Suzanne glanced up and met Matt's adoring, amber-colored eyes. He winked, a warm smile creeping across his boyish face. A wisp of blonde hair hung down over his forehead, but tonight it shone gold in the flickering firelight.

Each time she was with the 28-year-old minister she felt more comfortable. Yet each time she looked into his beckoning eyes, she drank in more love than she was able to offer in return. Matt was first a Christian which her husband would have to be. He was very good looking and had a strong measure of depth in his charm. He was exactly what she always dreamed she wanted in a lifetime mate. Would her caring someday grow to match the depth of his love for her? She hoped so.

Adam Wilder's deep voice broke into her thoughts. "How far above you and Ned was the plane do you think?"

Suzanne's brow wrinkled in serious consideration to the question posed by the town's unofficial mayor. Wilder, a prosperous cattle rancher, was also the owner of the local gas station and a popular restaurant called Adam's Rib. A good-natured, huskily-built man in his early fifties with olive skin and graying hair, Wilder could be easily spotted from a distance by the massive turquoise belt buckle and matching watch band he always wore. He was as proud of his American Indian heritage as he was of his lifelong citizenship in Hastings.

"Maybe 1000 feet" was Suzanne's considered opinion. "Although I can't be sure. We couldn't see anything at all, engulfed as we were by the stinging wind and swirling snow."

"Adam and I were in the middle of a fireside chess game, waiting for you, when we heard the plane overhead," interjected Matt, brushing a few cornbread crumbs from the lapel of his soft corduroy jacket. "The pilot had to be lower than 1000 feet. The whole cottage shook. Every window rattled. I really expected some of the hand-blown panes in this old parsonage to shatter under the stress."

"I can't think of a rancher within 100 miles of here who would venture out on a night like this. If he's away from his ranch, he'd stay away," concluded Wilder.

"Ned suggested that, if it were daylight, the pilot might seek out the Stevens Ranch airstrip..."

Adam shook his head. "Only the locals know about that field. Like I said, the locals wouldn't be out..."

Suzanne took a chance. "What's the story behind the Stevens Ranch?"

Adam looked at his watch thoughtfully. *Oh, no. Another put-off. What's with the Stevens legend anyway?*

"I guess we have a few minutes before the meeting. I'll give you a brief overview of the family that founded Hastings."

"Founded Hastings?" Suzanne was surprised.

"Yes. When Rufus Stevens came here,

Hastings was only a wide spot in the river where gold panners set up camp. The area boomed faster than it could garner a name. Although a gold miner himself, civic-minded Rufus took time to set up a school tent for the increasing influx of children in the area. After six months, the men in town pitched in and built a one-room school—which is your classroom now, Suzanne. The other eight classrooms were added one at a time through the years."

"How did Hastings get its name?" Matt asked.

"Hastings, the oldest son of Rufus Stevens, along with thirteen others, died of typhoid about the time a committee to name the town was formed. Naming the town after his son was an attempt to show appreciation to Stevens. . ."

Suzanne was puzzled. "I find a reluctance on some people's part to talk about the Stevens family . . ." She deliberately left her sentence unfinished.

Adam scowled. "I don't know why. The family left without skeletons in the closet."

"Left? When?" Suzanne asked.

"About 20 years ago. Rufus' two grandsons, Carl and Walter, owned the largest cattle spread in the area. When Walter was killed in a tragic hunting accident, his city-bred wife, who had always hated the isolated life here, packed up her two children and hightailed it back to San Francisco—'the cultural center of the West,' she called it."

"Does anyone live on the ranch now?" Suzanne inquired.

Adam leaned forward and rested his arms on the table. "Only a caretaker. The surviving brother, Carl, comes up once or twice a year to hunt. The widow and her children, who are grown by now, have never returned."

Finished, Adam sat back, carefully folded his napkin and placed it next to his empty chili bowl.

"That's all?" Suzanne asked in disbelief.

"That's all. But, by the look on your face, I'd say you were expecting the confirmation of a bit of gossip," observed the storyteller.

"No," Suzanne countered quickly. "To be truthful, I hadn't heard a word of the Stevens story. I was beginning to wonder if the family really existed."

"Oh, they existed all right," Wilder responded, tiredly. "And so does everlasting gossip in this small town. Right, Preacher?"

Suzanne turned her attention to Matt, who was obviously caught off guard. "Did I miss more than the chess game before dinner?"

"Not really," Matt hedged. Then throwing up his arms in frustration, he admitted, "I got one more telephone call from another well-meaning member who began almost apologetically. 'I shouldn't tell you this, Pastor, but I heard that Mr. Georges . . .' Then fed by his own rage, ended by demanding that I ask Mr. Georges to withdraw his church membership!

"Fortunately, I dutifully remembered rule number one—ministers may not show anger. I held my own until Adam showed up, then I opened up the valves and let it all pour out." Then reaching over and squeezing the rancher's forearm, Matt added, "Sorry about that, Old Man."

Adam lightened the dark turn of events with a chuckle. "No problem. My wife says church gossip gave her an ulcer. She stopped listening to it and the ulcer disappeared. When Caroline returns from visiting her sister in Sacramento, I'll send her over to give you the cure."

"Thanks, Adam. I wish it were that simple. It isn't. Gossip is just a symptom. It may be an age-old habit at Hastings Community Church, but that doesn't purify the stink it causes. It just reaffirms that most of the membership regards the church as an institution, a club, for the preservation of social identity in the community. The church, in Hastings at least, does not see itself as the Body of the continuing ministry of Jesus."

"I've always felt evangelism and Bible study were the foundation of the church," Suzanne declared. She quickly glanced toward Adam who nodded his agreement.

Matt could not control his excitement.

"Right on!" Then adding dramatically, "Then why is it I fail to get support for mid-week cottage Bible study groups? I get all kinds of flak if I fail to put a notice on the bulletin board stating that Mrs. Jones is now serving her sixth consecutive term on the board of the Ladies' Guild, or recognize in the weekly printed announcements the birth of a grandson to the chairman of the Board of Elders."

Adam took advantage of the young minister's pause. "Getting to the nitty-gritty—you're frustrated because the church members are dealing on a gossip level with Mr. Georges' trip to a faith healer, rather than on a Biblical level."

Matt shook his head affirmatively. "You're a master at peeling away the varnish and exposing the grain of the matter. I appreciate your friendship, Adam, and yours, too, Suzanne."

Then Matt reached out and joined hands with his two friends. "Lord, continue to strengthen our faith. Let our lights shine, leading others to the true purpose of Your church here in Hastings."

The mantel clock struck three-quarters past the hour. Matt reluctantly pushed back his chair. "Another rule. The minister is always first at every meeting. He looks like a slacker otherwise."

"Methinks our friend is feeling a bit sorry for himself," Suzanne teased.

Adam chuckled agreeably as he gave Matt an encouraging pat on the back. Then, while Adam quieted the fire and Matt blew out the candles on the table and on the buffet, Suzanne had time to reflect on Mr. Georges' boast that he'd visited a faith healer while on a recent trip and had watched as "Thomas," layed hands on him and miraculously healed a prior medically-documented hiatal hernia.

Mr. Georges bragged that his traveling companion took movies of the healing service, if proof was needed beyond his own statement that he no longer found it difficult to breathe or eat comfortably.

Her musing over, the trio donned their boots and heavy coats then headed toward the society room located in the rear of the church building. The purpose of tonight's meeting was to finalize plans for Friday's annual churchwide festival. The hubbub had been building for weeks. The Ladies' Guild was busily dabbing the last bit of glue on craft projects. Others were occupied labeling and pricing their frozen and canned fruits and vegetables and baking fresh pies, cakes, and breads. The teenagers had collected enough books to set up a next-to-new book corner, and the men were offering for the first time a "tool trade" booth.

Before the committee disbanded that night a muslin curtain would be hung from the ceiling, separating the lecturn from the rest of the room. The pews would be pushed back to the side walls and card tables and chairs would have turned the society room into the beginning of a tea shop.

Friday morning the decorating crew, food committee, and donors would arrive early to transform the church into a "Showcase of Harvest Blessings." People from neighboring communities would be there when the doors officially opened at noon.

By 8 P.M., the church coffers would be one year closer to construction of a social hall the size of an indoor basketball court.

Although the wind had died down, the snow was still falling heavily. Matt took Suzanne by the arm and pulled her close. When she looked up at him a snowflake landed on the tip of her pixie nose. They laughed together as Matt gently brushed it from her face. Suzanne thrust her hands into her fur-lined coat pockets.

It was then that she remembered Holly's money. Before she could decide whether or not to mention the matter to her companions, Matt stepped ahead to hold back a low, snow-laden bough. They continued in single file through the stand of tall snow-crested pines that separated the parsonage by 100 yards from the steepled, white-clapboard church that was almost as old as Hastings Elementary itself.

The three came out of the trees near the side

entrance of the church. They all saw it at the same time—a warm, red glow pulsating through the stained-glass windows near the altar area.

Suzanne stopped in her tracks.

"Oh, my God! The church is on fire!" Adam's anguished words were more prayerful than profane.

Matt sprinted toward the stairs as fast as his long legs could bound through two feet of snow.

"No! No!" Adam yelled. "Don't open that door. The fire will explode in your face!" Wilder ran after Matt who did not heed the words shouted at his back.

It happened so quickly that later Suzanne could not recall which happened first—Wilder tackling the young minister by his feet at the bottom of the wooden staircase or the explosion that erupted from somewhere deep inside the building. An explosion so forceful that the leaded windowpanes along the entire wall of the church shattered, catapulting missiles of jagged glass in all directions. Even in her state of shock, Suzanne's mind registered the screech of ripping glass along with the fact that the sharp-edged pieces made no sound when sinking like land-mines in the soft snow around her feet.

Suzanne instantly thought of the two men she cared about laying facedown in the snow, covered and surrounded by shards of glass.

"Don't move!" she screamed. "There's glass everywhere. I'm going for help."

Suzanne fled, running blindly through the snow toward the front of the church. *Lord, don't let me fall on broken glass. I must get help! Where? How?* Somehow she knew what she had to do before she finished her petition.

She darted up the front steps of the church, threw herself through the unlocked front door and dashed into the vestibule. She glanced quickly through the glass windows of the double doors into the nave proper.

Flames licked hungrily at the lectern and at the hand-stitched green paraments of the Trinity season that hung from the lectern and pulpit. Several pews were on fire, fed by the upholstered cushions that ran the length of each row.

Suzanne turned and instinctively grabbed the rope that hung in the far corner. She pulled on it with all her strength. The rope moved only inches. She released it and pulled on it again, harder. *No wonder this is a two-man job on Sunday mornings!*

Another thought struck her. *I don't even know if Matt and Adam are hurt—or if either is alive!*

Suzanne summoned all her strength and more. She pulled down on the rope, harder—again and again.

Finally, after what seemed an eternity, Suzanne heard the clapper hit the side of the church bell high in the church steeple—weakly at first, then stronger the second and third time. Pulling strained every muscle in Suzanne's arms. Again, she pulled the rope harder. The bell cried out louder and louder. Soon help would come. It had to!

Suddenly, the double doors behind her burst open and a dark form rushed through. It hit her with such force that the heavy rope ripped free from her gloved hands and she was thrown against the wall. Her head struck the edge of something sharp before she fell to the floor.

The last thing she remembered was the acrid smell of melting nylon and the sound of the church bell tolling softer and softer.

Chapter Three

Suzanne awoke in unfamiliar surroundings. She was in a bedroom, though not her own. Delicate pink rosebuds climbed the taffeta-grained wallpaper to the high ceiling above. The dormer windows, which told her that she was in a second-story room, were hung with lace curtains, much like the ones she saw in Europe the summer of her graduation from college.

Carefully, she sat up on her elbows and pulled back the raspberry down comforter covering the old-fashioned brass bed. The rose print on the underside of the comforter matched the wallpaper roses. *A guest room— but whose?* she asked herself as she sat up and put her bare feet on the soft throw rug at the bedside. The muscles in her arms ached.

Suzanne stood up. Only then did she notice the flannel-lined, pink satin "grandmother" nightgown she was wearing. The long sleeves and high collar were trimmed in heavy ecru lace. She was more than a guest—she was a royal guest!

She tiptoed to the window and looked out. The sky was clear, the color of bluebells at their best in the spring. Last night's fearful storm had been driven off over the next mountain range leaving Hastings securely pinned beneath a silent blanket of fresh snow. In the distance, the tip-tilted block of granite that formed the 11,000-foot peak to the east was covered with snow. Dark clouds hovered behind the summit like a naughty schoolboy behind his mother.

Suddenly, Suzanne felt light-headed. She raised her hand to her forehead and closed her eyes. There was a bandage at her hairline!

She hurried to the bed and sat down. It all came back—the explosion, the jagged glass in the snow, the pain of pulling on the bell rope.

Then—*Someone hit me! He came from inside the burning church! He didn't want me to call for help—he must have started the fire himself! I've got to warn Matt!*

Matt! Where is Matt? Where is Adam? Where am I?

Just then there was a soft knock on the door. Before Suzanne could respond, the door opened.

"Bessie! I wondered whose hospitality I was accepting. I'm glad it's yours."

Bessie, smiling at her patient's obvious good health, hurried across the room to Suzanne's side. The two greeted one another with a warm hug.

"You did give Ned and me a scare last night. It was Mr. Georges who found you unconscious in the church vestibule. The town is buzzing with the news that you saved the church from burning to the ground. Only the Lord Himself knows what caused that old gas furnace to explode the way it did."

Suzanne felt a flush fill her cheeks. She smiled only briefly, her mind set on the question uppermost in her mind. "How are Matt and Adam? I . . ."

"They're both fine," she replied, settling herself on the bed next to Suzanne. Then taking Suzanne's hand affectionately in her own, she said, "Minister Matt was here to see you earlier, around 10 A.M. He said to tell you that he'd be at the church if you feel well enough to walk over."

"I sure do. However, I need to go home first and shower. The smoke I smell is probably coming from my hair."

Mrs. Woloski laughed. Her rosy cheeks looked like two shiny apples. She wiped her hands on her butcher's apron.

"Ned said that's what you'd want to do. So, he called on your landlady after breakfast. She packed an overnighter for you and sent it back with a jar of your favorite—pomegranate jam. We insist that you spend the weekend with us."

Before Suzanne could protest, Bessie added, "Besides, the doctor said that you have a mild concussion and should take it easy for several days. He suggested you not stay alone."

"Doctor? Doctor Shaw? When did I see him?"

"He came here to the house after Ned and Mr. Georges carried you here and summoned him. He took a look at the menfolk, too. As I said, they're fine now, though they were shaken up last night. It could have been much worse for all of you."

Suzanne shivered. She saw again the dark form striking her hard enough to send her crashing against the wall, then leaving her to be swallowed up by the flames.

"Thank you, Bessie. I'd like to spend the weekend with you and in this lovely guest room. All the times I've been in your home, I never knew this room existed."

"It was our daughter's room."

"Daughter? I didn't know that you had a . . ." Suzanne caught her breath as the anguish of unrequited grief spread across the grandmotherly face near hers.

"I'm sorry. I didn't mean to..."

Bessie got up and walked to the window. She drew back the curtain and said matter-of-factly, "There's another search plane. This one's going too fast to spy anything on the ground smaller than Grant's Reservoir."

"Search plane?" she questioned. Her right temple began to throb.

"The Civil Air Patrol in Reno called the Wilder Ranch this morning wondering if anyone heard a single-engine plane in the area last night. A ranch foreman in Southern Oregon reported his boss overdue on a flight from California. Hastings is in direct line between two VORs, whatever that means."

Suzanne took a deep breath and relaxed. There was no way for that missing plane to be on a collision course with her life!

"I don't know what that means myself, Bessie. I've never been up in a light plane. The closest I've been to small aircraft is at the Reno Air Races."

If Suzanne had taken time to elaborate, she would have told Bessie that her day at the world's largest air race, on a beautiful autumn day more than a year ago, was the occasion of her first date with Matt. To mention it now would open the door to a conversation filled with questions she was unprepared to answer. Besides, she wanted to get dressed and get over to the church to talk with Matt.

Her friend was glad to see her when she arrived at the church about an hour later. She found Matt shoveling out debris along with several other men and teenaged boys. When he saw her he dropped his shovel and walked toward the front door where she waited. On the way he wiped his brow with a bright red and white handkerchief.

"Good afternoon, Sleeping Beauty," he grinned. "You look well-rested."

"It's almost worth the slight headache I have to get the attention the Woloskis are showering on me." Then looking around, she said, "This place is a mess!"

"You should have seen it before we started working a couple of hours ago. Once all this stuff is out we'll be able to assess the damage more accurately. The pews, of course, are a total loss," he sighed.

Suzanne smiled mischievously.

"It's an answer to prayer, Matt. You told me the other day that you wanted to preach to 'standing room only' crowds on Christmas Eve."

Matt's return volley was quick. "Except for you," he teased. "You may sit beside me behind the pulpit. We can't have you falling down and knocking your head against the wall again, can we?"

Suzanne turned her back and started to walk away, out of earshot of the other workers. Matt followed until they reached the outside steps. He took her gently by the arm.

She stopped and looked up into his questioning eyes.

"What is it?" he asked.

"I didn't fall last night, Matt. I was thrown down and left to die in the fire that was deliberately set."

Matt's face turned ashen. "Whatever makes you think that?"

"Not whatever, it's whoever—whoever flew out those double doors and slammed into me, then left me dizzy-brained on the floor."

"Any idea who?"

"Only that he got his jacket too close to the fire. I smelled melting nylon."

Matt was silent for a moment, then said confidentially, "I didn't want to think the worst when I checked the furnace room and found the gas lines had been loosened. Still, I think we stand a better chance of finding the culprit if we keep this information to ourselves."

"You're probably right. The church has enough troubles without having the members suspicious of one another. The person responsible will likely be the one least suspected. Meanwhile, the questioned reputation of others could linger unjustly for years."

"My, I didn't know you were a psychologist, too."

"Comes from being a preacher's kid. You ought to know how that feels."

"I certainly do. I feel as though I grew up in a fishbowl. I had as many tattlers to my parents as members who paid my father's salary."

Suzanne smiled. "We've also had as many prayer partners, which may be the reason we each turned out somewhat credible."

Their banter was interrupted by a pickup pulling up at the foot of the steps. "I heard the bad news only minutes ago, Pastor Owens," Mr. McArthur called from the cab. "I was shocked when Ollie over at Western Auto told me about the fire. A full house out at the motel kept me from driving in for the meeting last night." Then, looking directly at Suzanne, he added, "Sorry I missed all the excitement."

Suzanne suddenly thought of the money still in her coat pocket. She walked down the steps to the mud-splattered truck, carefully withdrawing the crumpled brown bag from its hiding place.

She handed the bag to Mr. McArthur through the cab window with the explanation, "The janitor and I found this in Holly's desk. Please, don't be too hard on her for forgetting to bank it."

Mr. McArthur looked at Suzanne. It was clear, too late, that he had no idea what Suzanne was talking about. Suzanne tried to quell the sudden sick feeling in the pit of her stomach.

By that time, the motel owner had the bag

open. He reached in with his oversized, claw-like hands and yanked out the roll of bills. He stared at the wad of green just long enough for Suzanne to see a wave of red move up from his collar and erupt across his face in large crimson splotches.

He shoved the money back in the bag and revved his truck engine. Suzanne stepped back as Mr. McArthur gunned the motor and peeled out, spraying snow and mud in his wake.

Matt hurried down the steps two at a time. "What was that all about?" he asked, helping Suzanne brush the soggy globules from her coat hemline.

"I don't know, but I think I just committed a most unprofessional act. Pray, seriously, that I'm the only one who suffers for it."

Matt quipped, "I think that the last 24 hours have been too much for all of us. I wonder how many remember that today is Thanksgiving?"

"I remember. That's why I'm here," sounded a familiar voice.

The two spun around and saw Adam Wilder coming down the church steps.

"I just retraced our walk from the parsonage. We are standing here now because the Holy Spirit was watching over us last night."

Adam rested his hands on his hips and continued. "I think I'd better send in a couple of my ranch hands to help get the heavy debris cleaned out and the walls washed down. We're likely to have another storm in a couple of days."

"It would be appreciated..."

"Hey, Pastor, church maintenance is the members' responsibility. All we have to do is educate the rest of the 'let George do its' in the congregation."

Matt smiled weakly, as if he still carried the weight of the world on his shoulders.

"Now, the main reason I stopped by was to invite the two of you to an old-fashioned Thanksgiving dinner at the restaurant. Caroline's home and eager to get into her kitchen. She's had the turkey basting in the oven for a couple of hours already."

"We'd love to come," they agreed in unison.

Then Suzanne asked, "I thought you were closed for the whole weekend—with Caroline at her sister's and the holiday..."

"We are. Fact is, we've invited so many to share this special meal with us, including the Woloskis," he said, nodding to Suzanne, "that we decided to fix dinner in town rather than have everyone fight the snowy roads to the ranch. Also, we've invited two strangers to break bread with us."

"Strangers?" asked Matt. "You don't know any."

Adam's voice took on a serious tone. "That plane we heard overhead last night? Could have been two men on their way to Oregon.

Theirs is the only aircraft unaccounted for in the storm area. The Civil Air Patrol suggested to the relatives that they set up search headquarters in Hastings.

"The CAP captain in Reno asked my help in getting the center established. The first two members of the search team, a nephew of one of the men and a pilot friend of the other man in the missing plane, are arriving at Hastings Airfield in 15 minutes. I'm on my way to pick them up now."

The heaviness returned to Suzanne's heart.

"Who were . . . are the men in the missing plane? Who are the men you're picking up?"

Adam grinned. "No one I know, I'm sure. But since you're so interested, why don't you ride out with me? You're a prettier welcoming committee than I am by far."

"No, no, I didn't mean . . ." Suzanne sputtered.

"Why don't you?" Matt encouraged. "We're about ready to call it a day here at the church anyway. While you and Adam are running your errand of mercy I'll go back to the parsonage and clean up. We'll meet at Adam's Rib, in say, about an hour?"

Adam glanced at his watch. "That would suit Caroline perfectly. She likes to serve dinner the moment it's ready. It will also give our guests time to get settled at Winter's Inn before dinner."

Then, with a low, sweeping bow, Adam announced with mock haughtiness, "Your carriage awaits you, miss, as I do your company."

Suzanne did not feel that she could refuse Adam's well-intended invitation, even though her headache seemed to be growing worse. And there was the outside chance that the ride would do her good.

Getting off her feet did make a difference. Her headache disappeared as they drove along the winding road through a forest of snow-dipped evergreens that appeared loosely chained together in places by fresh deer tracks in the snow. Soon, she was thinking less of her own problems and more and more of the magnificent beauty of God's creation surrounding them. The Sierra Nevadas—covering almost as much territory as occupied by the French, Italian, and Swiss Alps combined—also contained canyons of 4,000- to 5,000-foot depths and a few chasms deeper than the Grand Canyon. Each time they rounded a curve a fresh, panoramic view held her breathless. Birds soared over meadows where winter-coated deer foraged near crystal-glazed mountain streams.

When the airport came into view, Suzanne's meandering mind returned to the matter at hand. "What is the Civil Air Patrol and how does it set up a search headquarters?"

Adam smiled. "Questions your eighth graders will be asking next Monday morning?"

"And Teacher better know the answers,"

she responded with a quick wink.

"First of all, the Civil Air Patrol is one of the volunteer organizations that the Air Force utilizes in searching for missing private aircraft. Our nearest unit is in Reno."

"How is this private search team related to the CAP in Reno?"

"Captain Marston, in Reno, will coordinate the search from his office at Hamilton Air Force Base. Remember, the missing plane could have landed almost anywhere in Nevada, southeast Oregon, or southwest Idaho, depending on how long the craft stayed up. Marston's now busy contacting units in the other areas, which in turn will instigate their own searches."

"I'm beginning to understand," she replied slowly.

"All that is really known is that the plane took off from John Wayne Airport in Southern California and flew to Stockton in Northern California. The men refueled and checked weather. They were told that a storm was moving in from the northwest fairly rapidly but it had not reached where they were going—to a ranch somewhere near the Oregon-Idaho border."

"Hastings is nowhere near that area."

"In a way it is. Let me explain."

"I wish I'd brought my pad and pencil."

"You'll remember what little we know about the events that led up to the craft's disappearance. Frankly, all that's left to tell is that sometime later, the pilot radioed for weather conditions at three alternate locations, two in Idaho, and one in eastern Nevada. He asked for information through a radio communication point located near Reno. This communication tower is known as Reno VOR. Hastings lies in a straight line between Reno VOR and the Rome VOR near their destination."

"VOR?" Suzanne asked thoughtfully.

Adam flipped his left-turn blinker and slowed his four-wheel-drive vehicle. He was quiet until he had turned onto the narrow road that ended near a row of buildings alongside the freshly snowplowed runway.

"Before I answer your question, see that metal structure at the far left? That's the hangar where I keep my Cessna Turbo 210 in the winter. In the summertime, I keep Eight-Kilo-Mike at my airstrip on the ranch."

"I've never ridden in a single-engine plane..."

"We'll fix that soon enough. Meanwhile, I want you to understand the importance of VOR. It's a term used in the airplane world and stands for 'visual omni range.' There are VOR stations throughout the U.S. They're used by commercial and private planes for navigational purposes."

Adam coasted to a stop in front of his hangar. He turned off the engine and continued his explanation. "Based on where and when the pilot called for weather and upon how much fuel he probably had left, Reno calculated how far the pilot was capable of flying if all went well."

"Is there a special reason why the pilot would choose to circle Hastings looking for a landing spot over, say, a town east of here in the less treacherous flatlands?"

"That is a mystery. It's possible, in fact probable, that the plane we heard over Hastings last night was not the missing plane. But for those two men walking toward us—it's a place to begin."

Suzanne looked up, startled. She squinted into the bright sunlight and studied the approaching men. The shorter and older of the two had a slight limp. He wore a navy blue baseball cap with gold letters on it, a heavy leather flight jacket, Levis, and cowboy boots. He carried a United Airlines flight bag and seemed to have a sandy complexion. It was hard to tell what was behind the oversized dark glasses.

The other walked with his square shoulders back and with an unusually even gait. A military academy graduate? She guessed his age at about 30. She smiled to herself. *A city boy. Suit, overcoat, dress shoes—and carrying a briefcase.* As he walked closer, she added, *Tall, dark-skinned, and handsome, just like in the movies. I bet his eyes are dark and flash-*

ing, his smile disarming.

Adam Wilder stepped from his vehicle and walked toward the two men. Suzanne watched as the three shook hands cordially. Adam turned and pointed in her direction. The two men nodded and headed toward the Suburban.

The rancher opened the front door on the passenger side. "Suzanne, I'd like you to meet the search team—Paul Schroeder, the pilot who landed in that Bonanza, parked over there, just before we rounded the last bend in the road. Watching him land would have been a beautiful sight for you to see."

She took Paul's firm handshake. "It's nice to meet you," she spoke sincerely. "We pray for your success in the search."

"Thank you." He sounded surprised at her concern.

"Who do you know in the missing plane?"

"Bill Daniels, my close friend. Although both men have licenses, it was Bill's plane. He was probably in the left seat."

"Left seat?"

"That means, Miss Flynn, that Bill Daniels was the pilot in command," came the answer from Paul's companion, as he extended his hand to Suzanne.

Suzanne put her hand into his. He grasped it tightly. She allowed her eyes to move up slowly to meet his. She found them the color of polished brown stones on the bottom of a mountain stream. She began to tremble as she waited to hear the stranger's name.

He glanced down at her through thick, black lashes. A slow smile rippled across his face, exposing a row of perfect white teeth. "The passenger in the plane was my uncle, Carl Stevens, owner of the Stevens Ranch, located outside of Hastings. I couldn't tell you in which direction, though. It's been years since my father's death at which time my mother took the family to live in San Francisco. I haven't been back since."

"I know." Suzanne felt her heartbeat quicken, then skip a beat. The dark-eyed businessman looked at her quizzically.

Suzanne quickly asked, "Then, you are . . ."

"Leif Stevens, the second member of the search team. Hopefully, there will be more searchers arriving soon. Among them, my fiancee, Jessica Jacobs."

Chapter Four

"It's exactly 9 A.M. Time to get this meeting underway if we expect to be in the air the moment the weather clears." Adam got everyone's attention.

"First of all, I want to thank each and every one of you for responding to our call for help. Those of us committed to this search fully realize the sacrifices being made in the homes represented here this Friday morning—a workday for some, the middle of a holiday weekend for others."

Suzanne watched from her counter-top seat

at the back of her classroom as Adam, perched casually on the corner of her desk at the front of the room, motioned to Matt.

Matt stepped forward and bowed his head. Everyone else in the room did the same as Matt prayed aloud. "Father in heaven, cover each person in this room with Your divine protection as we set out in search of the missing craft. Direct us where You will. Give us eyes to see what You intend. Keep safe and warm those for whom we search. Above all, Thy will be done. We pray in the name of Your Son, Jesus Christ. Amen."

"Amen," intoned a chorus of mixed voices.

Matt slipped into a seat near the front of the room as Adam once again took control of the meeting.

"Allow me to preface our strategy session by repeating what I told Stevens and Schroeder earlier at breakfast. The plane that flew over Hastings night before last may or may not have been the Carl Stevens craft. Nevertheless, Reno CAP had five planes up at daybreak Thanksgiving morning searching the area around and north of Hastings. Although the weather was clear, the heavy snowfall the night before could have easily shrouded their plane, which was white with brown trim. CAP planes searched both morning and afternoon."

Adam cleared his throat. "In addition, Idaho and Oregon were notified. A number of planes were aloft by 9 A.M. in both states. You see, although it seems that we are entering the search late, the most likely air routes traveled by the missing plane have already been scanned at least once. Unfortunately, there's not been a single sighting of a likely downed craft.

"There are three possible fates to the plight of the Hastings mystery plane. First, it could have landed safely somewhere on a private strip and the pilot is unaware that there is a full-scale Western Region search in progress. After all, he did not file a flight plan prior to takeoff. Therefore he is not obligated to notify authorities at the completion of his flight.

"Secondly, the plane could have landed safely and the men are either waiting at the craft to be rescued from difficult terrain or are trying to hike out to civilization on their own.

"Finally, we must face the possibility a fatal crash occurred and that despite all search efforts we may not find the crash sight until the spring thaw."

A cloud of silence hung over the room. Everyone there knew the odds of doing storm battle over the High Sierra. However, when Adam spoke again, it was with hope in his voice.

"I have a report that seven planes are already up this morning in Idaho. Two in Oregon. I do not have a report from the Nevada CAP yet. We have three planes committed to today's search here in Hastings. If needed, we have two additional planes that will be mechanically ready by tomorrow."

Adam glanced up from his clipboard and pointed to the burly rancher in the second row. "Jake McCafferty, Mr. Georges will be your spotter this morning. You'll take the area southeast, the Strawberry Pass area."

He waited for an assenting nod before turning to Kevin Johnson, owner of the Bar Double Q. "Leif Stevens will spot for you. Cover the Stevens Ranch area with a fine-toothed comb. Although several ranch hands rode the ranch's fence line yesterday, they naturally miss the hidden terrain in the deep canyons.

"Paul, I'll spot for you this morning. By this afternoon other members of your party should be here to relieve some of us. Several of the men will need the afternoon to haul in aviation fuel from Westbrook. Four senior high boys have volunteered to help pump fuel from 55-gallon drums into the planes late this afternoon. Should we need to search tomorrow, we want the planes ready to go at daybreak."

Adam paused for a moment before making an observation. "The ways of God are often a mystery to mortals. However, keep in mind, had not the church fire cancelled 'Harvest of Blessings,' which annually draws hundreds of visitors from distant communities, most of us would have been busy unsnarling traffic, cooking for the spaghetti supper or working the booths. We would have been unavailable to help organize a search this soon."

There were mumbled words of agreement among those seated among the rows of desks. Adam tapped on the teacher's desk with his pen. The room grew quiet once more.

"Miss Flynn," Adam said, looking over the heads of the assembled group of about 25 people. Many heads turned to follow Adam's gaze. She noticed that Leif Stevens was one who turned and was looking at her.

She kept her eyes on Adam, however, as he asked, "Would you please find me some map tacks. I want to display an aeronautical chart of the search area on the bulletin board."

Suzanne was grateful for the opportunity to slip away from the eye of attention. She lifted her coat from the row of pegs at the back door and left the room. After looking up and down the arcade for Ned's familiar cleaning cart, she recalled that he'd cleaned the rooms the night before Thanksgiving. This was a holiday for him. She hurried toward the main storage room, looking for the proper key on her key ring as she went.

She was surprised to find the door ajar and the light on. She pushed and it squeaked open. Ned was hunched over an open box of records in the middle of the floor. From where she stood she could read the neatly felt-penned words "Student Admission Applications" on the side of the carton.

Ned looked up. "Shut that door quick as you can, please. This room's got no heat."

Nonplussed, Suzanne asked, "Do you need help looking for something?"

"No" was his one-word reply, as he grabbed hold of the center support post to help pull himself up. A manila folder was tucked under his left arm.

"What can I do for you?" he asked, picking up a second folder waiting on a shelf near the door.

"Ah...I need a package of map tacks."

"Right behind you on the second shelf," he said, starting to leave.

"Ned...where are you going with those confidential files?"

"That's confidential," he replied gruffly, shutting the door behind him.

Suzanne gasped in dismay. Just then, Ned reopened the door, stuck his head in, and winked. Then he was gone for good.

Suzanne picked up the box of tacks and returned to her classroom in time to hear the handlebar-mustached Kurt Schmidt, publisher of the weekly *Hastings Gazette*, say, "It's said that a miner down near Oak Creek heard a plane pass over low—he's sure the plane was to the south of his cabin."

"Heading to or coming from the south?" Adam prodded.

Suzanne was startled to hear a familiar voice

interject. "Never mind. I'll check it out." It was Sheriff Blake.

What's he doing here? He must have sneaked in while I was out in the shed with Ned. What's he doing in Hastings? Could his interest be the fire? Who told him it wasn't an accident?

Suzanne heard Adam say something about the ladies fixing a noon potluck at Adam's Rib, complete with fresh pies rerouted from Harvest Blessings. He then dismissed the group.

There was the shuffle of chairs and the buzz of conversation. She was still concentrating on the sheriff's enigmatic presence when she heard a voice close to her ear inquire, "What's keeping you on the ground this morning, Miss Flynn?"

She whirled around to find Leif's face close to hers, his dark eyes impishly searching hers for an answer.

"Probation. Today's my last day, if I'm a good girl," she replied easily, touching the place on her forehead where the bandage used to be, then running her beautifully manicured fingers through her long hair that shimmered when caught by the morning light streaming through the window.

"May I ask a favor of you...if you're not too busy?"

"Sure. I'll do what I can," Suzanne's blue eyes sparkled.

"A pilot friend is flying Jessica up. They

should be at the airport at 11:30 this morning. Could you...would you pick her up?"

Suzanne opened her mouth but the words would not come. The heaviness she felt when she heard the plane overhead the night before last returned with a thud.

"If it's inconvenient, I certainly understand..."

"No...no," was her stuttered reply. "Of course I'll meet her plane. I'm sure she's a very nice person."

Why did I say that? Suzanne felt a warm flush fill her cheeks. *What difference does it make whether Miss Jacobs is nice or not? She's Leif's fiancée—that's all that matters.*

"You may count on me picking up Miss Jacobs and the pilot. I'll bring them into town to Winter's Inn and see that they're at Adam's Rib to meet you for lunch."

"Thanks..." His remark seemed unfinished. He took his eyes from Suzanne's and quickly surveyed the room. "Is everyone in Hastings always this accommodating, or is this Sunday-best for strangers?"

The sparkle in Suzanne's eyes hardened to a flash. "Metropolitan indifference is not practiced here, nor is rudeness part of 'small town culture.' "

Leif's startled eyes met hers. "I'm sorry. I didn't mean..." He reached out and put his hand gently on her shoulder. "I didn't mean to be critical. I was unprepared for the warmth extended to us by everyone. It's caught me a little by surprise."

"What did you expect from a small community of people who must team play every season of the year to survive?"

Leif was quiet for a moment—long enough for Suzanne to hear her own voice ringing sourly in her ears. She looked up at a man who was no longer smiling down at her.

"Forgive me," she apologized. "I'm the one who's rude—not these wonderful people who not long ago welcomed me as warmly as they are now welcoming you. Their caring is quite sincere, I assure you."

"I confess," Leif offered in explanation, "for years, I heard that Hastings was a small, backward area, with few redeeming social graces."

Suddenly, Suzanne remembered that Leif had been the young child whisked from Hastings by a mother bitterly unhappy with isolated mountain life, and a lifestyle that had claimed her husband.

"Shall we start over?" Suzanne suggested with a soft smile. "We've both been under enormous strain the last few days." She offered her hand to Leif.

He took it quickly into his own. Suzanne felt her heart flutter, just as it had done the moment of their first meeting at the airport.

"Let's do," he whispered, holding her hand

a moment longer before letting it slip from his. Then his brow furrowed with concern. "The strain you've been under? I hope it hasn't been due to the plane..."

"Oh, no! I'll explain later," she said to close their conversation. Matt was coming toward them.

"It gives me a meeting to look forward to," Leif voiced eagerly as Matt reached them.

Leif excused himself and Matt was about to say his first words to Suzanne when Jake McCafferty walked up and interrupted. "You got something to do with Georges riding with me, Preacher?" His tone was accusing.

Matt bristled and looked Mr. McCafferty straight in the eye. He took a moment to harness his anger before asking, "You have a problem taking Brother Georges with you, Jake?" In contrast, Matt's tone was that of a caring counselor.

"I feel uncomfortable with some of the things Mr. Georges has been involved with lately."

Suzanne watched the color drain from Matt's face as he tried to control the thoughts in his mind, the movements of his tongue.

She closed her eyes and prayed for the strength that must be Matt's at this moment.

When she opened them, she noticed that Matt had placed his hand understandingly on Jake's shoulder. "Don't judge him before he's had the opportunity to speak for himself,

Brother. Only the Lord knows why you were assigned together this morning. I had nothing to do with it. Therefore, take it as a sign that it was supposed to be. Perhaps it's an opportunity to witness."

Jake's temper cooled considerably. "Okay, we'll have it *His* way this morning. *You* take it out of God's hands this afternoon." With that, he turned on his heel and left.

Matt shrugged his shoulders. "Not even God wins all the time."

"Don't despair, Matt. God's always in control."

"I know. I have to remember that with every shovelful. And speaking of church renovation, I'd better get over to my own project. See you at lunch?"

"Sure," she replied, reminded once again of Jessica Jacobs, the guest she would be bringing with her.

After the room cleared, she straightened it a little, placed a fresh pad of paper and a newly sharpened pencil on her desk for Adam. She unplugged the near-empty coffeepot and prepared it for a fresh brew for the afternoon briefing. Finally, Suzanne was ready to walk the three blocks to Bessie and Ned Woloski's to get her car keys.

She was locking her classroom door when she heard a sweet young voice call out disappointedly, "Am I too late to help, Miss Flynn?"

Suzanne looked up and smiled. Holly was coming along the arcade toward her. Yes, she was definitely thinner. Her long, blonde hair, usually the color of summer wheat, had lost its luster. *I wonder if she's had a checkup from Dr. Shaw lately?*

"Am I delighted to see you!" She put her arm lovingly around her prize student's shoulder. "I've been thinking about you a lot the last couple of days."

"Have I done something wrong?"

"Of course not, dear. Never mind that now. You've come to help?"

"Yes, but it looks as if I'm too late." Her green eyes betrayed a sadness that startled Suzanne.

"Maybe not, Holly. I need your help. Would you ride out to the airport with me to meet a plane bringing two more searchers?"

"How is that helping?"

Suzanne swallowed, waiting for the right words. When none came, she blurted out the truth.

"I'm uncommonly nervous about meeting these particular people. I'll feel more comfortable if you're there to support me."

Holly's green eyes brightened slightly. Suzanne's sincerity had not escaped her quick mind. "I'd love to go with you. My parents are not expecting me until mid-afternoon."

"Good. Then we'll have lunch together at the potluck." Suzanne did not try to conceal her relief or her joy. She prayed silently for the opportunity—and soon—to gain some insight into Holly's troubled spirit.

As they walked toward Woloskis', Suzanne's mind wandered long enough to form some questions. *What kind of woman is Leif attracted to? And what's special about Jessica Jacobs? She must be extremely attractive to attract the handsome Leif Stevens. I hope she's as friendly as he has proven to be.*

As the two rounded the last corner and started down Sycamore Street, Holly slipped in the slushy snow. Suzanne's reflexes were quick. She caught Holly around the waist before she fell. Suddenly, Holly screamed with pain and pushed Suzanne's arm away from her side.

"Holly! What's the matter?" She threw her arms around Holly's shoulders to steady the trembling young teen.

She needed help. Suzanne glanced down the street toward Ned and Bessie's. She looked just in time to see Sheriff Blake's car pull away from Woloskis' house. The sheriff was not alone in the car. Ned, wearing his familiar red wool cap, was slouched in the caged back seat!

Chapter Five

Bessie answered Suzanne's first hard knock on the front door.

"Gracious! What's the matter with Miss Holly? She's pale as a winter moon."

Without waiting for an answer, she helped Suzanne walk Holly to the plaid sofa in front of the fireplace.

Once Holly was tucked under a warm comforter, Suzanne turned to her friend. "Oh, Bessie!" she blurted out. "We saw Sheriff Blake drive off with Ned locked in the back seat of his patrol car. Ned couldn't have started the fire. He saved my life! What are we going to do?"

"What are you babbling about, girl? That concussion has really scrambled your brain. Of course Ned didn't start the fire. He has business at the county seat. The sheriff's giving him a ride down the mountain. They'll be back before dark."

"County seat? What's the matter?"

"He's just checking some things out... before he says anything to anyone."

"Why... why was he riding in the back seat—like a prisoner?" she asked, still unconvinced of Ned's status of freedom.

"The arthritis in his leg is bothering him. Ned wanted to stretch out during the long ride." Then, wiping her hands on her ever-present apron, she nodded toward the frail figure on the sofa and whispered, "We'd better tend to the little injured bird we have in hand."

"I'm fine, I really am, Mrs. Woloski," Holly insisted in a thin voice.

"The color is coming back to her cheeks," noted Suzanne, placing her hand gently on the girl's forehead. "I don't believe she has a fever."

"What caused her to pale so?" Bessie asked as if the popular eighth-grader were not present to speak for herself.

"She slipped in the snow. It was when I grabbed her around her waist to keep her from falling that she screamed in agony. I didn't squeeze her hard enough to hurt her."

"I must have gotten a catch in my side. It happens to lots of people," offered Holly, who made no move to lift her head from the pillow.

"We'd better give her folks a call. They may want Dr. Shaw to look at her before taking her home," Bessie suggested.

"No! No! Please don't call my dad. He's . . . he's too busy this weekend," Holly begged. "And it's for sure, I don't want Dr. Shaw to examine me!" Holly's eyes pleaded with Suzanne.

"All right, dear," Suzanne agreed soothingly. "We won't do anything without your permission."

Bessie nodded to Suzanne. "Let's let her rest for a few minutes. Come into the kitchen with me. We'll fix some hot chocolate to drink in front of the fire before you go about your chores. We'll all feel better then."

Once behind the closed kitchen door, Bessie spoke softly. "You leave her here with me when you go. There's more hurting that child than her physical body."

"I know," Suzanne sighed, her mind flashing back to her recent unpleasant encounter with Holly's father.

"She may talk to me when you're gone. I'm safe. Holly looks up to you. She may fear you'd be disappointed in her if you knew what she's hiding from us."

"You may be right." She marveled at Bessie's acumen for child psychology.

"Whatever happens, Bessie, don't call her parents without her permission. She's not up to handling her father if he's in a disagreeable mood."

"I understand. Come back here before going to the potluck at noon. By then, we could have enough information from Holly to know what to do next."

A few minutes later, Suzanne was in her yellow compact car driving the main road out of town toward the airport and the highway beyond. Although the road was freshly plowed, she drove slowly, admiring the beautiful scenery. As she neared the airport turnoff, she looked up into the blue sky, dotted now with puffy clouds, and watched as a speck in the distance became a graceful, broad-winged, mechanical bird descending leisurely toward Mother Earth.

How wonderful it must be to fly! To sail among the frothy clouds, to look down upon the winding rivers, lush valleys, and layered rock formations God created just for us. How very special we the human race are!

She was alongside the airstrip when the plane glided to a smooth landing. As soon as it came to a full stop, Suzanne stepped from the warmth of her small car and walked in the 15-degree weather toward the two people climbing out of the cockpit.

Jessica Jacobs would have stood out in a crowd of hundreds. She was boyishly slim and tall—almost as tall as Leif. Her hair, silver-blonde, was cut fashionably to curl under at the shoulder line. And from several yards away, Suzanne recognized Jessica's pant suit as a designer cashmere. The color was light chocolate with a white mohair turtleneck sweater under the tailored jacket. Her ensemble was set off by gold loop earrings and at least a half dozen jingling gold bracelets. Surprisingly, Jessica was not wearing an engagement ring.

Suzanne introduced herself to Jessica, then to Leonard Coatsworth, the pilot. His first remark was, "Is this all there is to Hastings Airport?"

"Yes, it is. Is there something more that you require, Mr. Coatsworth? If so, several of the ranchers in the area have their own planes and airstrips. Perhaps one of them will have what you need."

Her remark definitely raised the visitors' eyebrows. However, it did not seem to bring Hastings up to even the poverty level in Jessica's mind.

"Lead on, Miss Flynn. Leif phoned last night and said he was all wrong about this place. So far, I'd say he's been sniffing too much high-altitude fresh air."

Suzanne smiled, pleased that Leif had abandoned his mother's negative view of Hastings and its residents. Exhilarated, a heady confidence swept over her. She'd take on Jessica and her snobbish airs!

"Then get ready to become intoxicated yourselves," Suzanne said decisively, with a welcoming smile. "I guarantee the scenery between here and town is the most breathtaking short of heaven."

"First," scowled Leonard, "we've got to figure out how to get six pieces of luggage in, or on top of, that little Rabbit of yours."

Suzanne carried tie-downs in the trunk, so it didn't take long to secure the heavy suitcases on the roof luggage rack. Suzanne figured that at least one of the suitcases had to belong to Leif, as he'd arrived with only a single change of clothes—another business suit. When notified early Thanksgiving morning of his uncle's missing plane, Leif was on his way back to California from a Denver business meeting, he had told her. He and the pilot simply changed course for Hastings.

Suzanne giggled to herself. *Wait until she sees how Leif's dressed this morning—borrowed Levis, plaid shirt, cowboy boots, and a fleece-lined jacket—none of them exactly the right size.*

The pilot and Jessica talked exclusively to one another on the way to town. Under the circumstances, Suzanne was happy with her role as taxi driver. She found it informative to keep quiet and listen. Suzanne learned that Jessica fully expected the search to conclude today, so that she and Leif could return to San Francisco in time for an opera benefit Saturday evening. Although she was not fond of the opera, it was an important evening for her career-wise, she told "Len" while checking her eye makeup in a jeweled compact mirror.

Suzanne got the impression that Len was a close friend of Leif's. Both being aerospace engineers, she learned he and Leif met while in Houston working on the space program. Leif accepted an upward career change and returned to California two years ago. Len soon followed and the two resumed their close ties.

The two visitors stopped talking when a deer unexpectedly bounded across the road in front of Suzanne's car. She slowed, and all three watched the graceful doe bounce effortlessly through the snow to join a small herd in the meadow to the left of the road. From then until they reached Winter's Inn, Jessica and Len concentrated on scanning the snowy fields for signs of more wildlife. The two were genuinely delighted with the tally of two sprinting jackrabbits, one stalking cougar, and a preening hawk sitting on a tree limb that overhung the roadway.

When Suzanne left the couple in front of Winter's Inn, there was a sparkle in Jessica's eyes that hadn't been there before

their journey through nature's wonderland—
or, maybe the sparkle was in anticipation of
seeing her love, Leif Stevens. Suzanne hurriedly said her good-byes to the two and got
back into her car. *Why should it make a difference why Jessica's eyes sparkled. Leif's
lovelife was not her affair.*

Two minutes later, Suzanne pulled up in
front of the Woloskis' to keep her appoint-
ment with Bessie, and a potluck date with
Holly. It was almost an afterthought that she
remembered Matt's eagerness to see her at
noon.

She stepped briskly up the front walk and
reached the porch when the storm door flew
open—nearly knocking her over.

"She's gone! Holly slipped out about twenty
minutes ago while I was in the kitchen tidying
up. I shouldn't have left her alone," Bessie
wailed, berating herself. "I should have
known she'd fly like a wounded robin once
I suspected the truth!"

Chapter Six

Suzanne stepped through the door and caught sight of Matt sitting alone at a small table in front of the screened waitress station. He nodded to the empty chair next to him. She smiled, then unobtrusively made her way among the tables to the place he'd saved for her. On the way she noticed that most of the search team had finished what appeared to have been a delicious meal.

"Ready for lunch?"

"No, thanks. I'm not hungry. Matt, I've got to talk to you!" The tone of her voice conveyed its own urgency as she slipped into the place across from the tired-looking young minister.

"Is the matter professional or personal?" he inquired half-heartedly, finishing off the last bite of blackbottom pie.

"Both."

Matt looked up, alerted. "I'm sorry. I didn't mean to sound flippant. I'm ready to listen, as long as it's you."

The lightly-etched lines of Matt's face that bespoke his good-natured spirit appeared deeply eroded, the by-product of exhaustion. She hesitated, unwilling to add to his burden.

He reached out and took her hand. "Come on, Suzanne. I know what you're thinking. Don't insult me by trying to protect me from one more crisis. It's time I had something to chew on other than dead-end clues as to who tried to burn down the church."

"Okay," she smiled. "This is very confidential. Should we go somewhere else?"

"I don't think so," he said, glancing around the room. "No one's paying attention to us. Tell me—before Adam starts the briefing."

Suzanne quickly shared the story of the found money in Holly's desk. She reminded Matt of Mr. McArthur's rage when she gave him the money and finally, she told him of the incident that led to Holly's panicked flight from Woloski's home.

Matt shook his head in disbelief. "That poor

child. More than anyone, I should have been sensitive to her needs. I'm her pastor, yet I saw nothing."

"Matt, stop it! Being a pastor does not make you God—all-seeing, all-knowing."

"How well I realize that, Suzanne."

"Matt, I . . ."

"Where is Holly now—any idea? Maybe we can still help."

"Not a clue. Holly doesn't want to be found. There's no use looking. She has many girl friends, but I doubt if any have her confidence in this matter."

"What does Bessie suspect is the truth?"

"That's another mystery, Matt. As distraught as she was, Bessie would not tell me. She just walked around the living room, wringing her hands, crying, 'Wait 'til Ned comes home. I can't say anything until we know what he found out. Just pray nothing happens to Holly before then.' "

Just then, Adam tapped on his water glass to gain the group's attention. As Adam shuffled his notes, Matt whispered, "I know how to find Holly this afternoon, without her even suspecting that I'm looking for her."

"Thank you, Matt . . ."

Suddenly, out of the corner of her eye, Suzanne caught a glimpse of movement to her right. She turned her head and saw Martha Pettijohn step out from behind the screened waitress station. She walked toward the kitchen carrying an empty coffeepot. Suzanne sensed by the smirk on Martha's face that Widow Pettijohn had overheard every word she and Matt had uttered!

Suzanne closed her eyes as her head began to swim in circles. *What have I done? Whatever plagues Holly, I've compounded it at every turn. Please, Lord, send Your angels to protect Holly—especially from well-meaning me!*

She glanced at Matt. He was watching the kitchen door, a grim expression on his face.

"It's confirmed," Adam began. "The Stevens plane is missing and is thought to be the mystery plane that flew over Hastings Thanksgiving Eve. There is no way to know in which direction or how far the plane flew before it was forced to land. We do know that it is extremely cold out there, dipping to below zero at night. Hope for survival lessens by the hour."

He walked quickly over to the makeshift bulletin board. "This morning's cursory search sadly yielded only the sighting of a pickup abandoned by hunters early in the season. We've marked the spot on the map, as we want all foreign objects noted upon the return of every flight.

"Our assigned search area is vast, overwhelming if the stakes were not two human lives. Because time is of the essence, we must tighten our search organization. We'll hold our briefings here after meals to save precious time. We appreciate the use of Suzanne's classroom this morning, but here, at the cafe, we also have access to a telephone and 24-hour use of the room, if necessary. We have to face the fact, also, that this search may continue into Monday, which is a school day."

Matt leaned over and whispered in Suzanne's ear. "I'll see you later. I've got to get back to work." He got up and quietly slipped out the side door.

"Pilots, before you leave this room to begin your afternoon search, I want each of you to list his plane number and spotter's name on this chart." Pointing to the posted, lined chart, he added emphatically, "Also list the agreed-upon area that you will be searching. We don't want any midair collisions."

"How are you dividing the search areas this afternoon?" asked Jake.

"I've talked with Reno CAP. They've agreed to release this area." He circled a large area of the High Sierra around Hastings with his black marker. "I've divided our area into 15-square-mile grids, and have given each grid a number. It will take about an hour to carefully cover one grid, going back and forth, slightly overlapping each trip.

"The winds aloft are tricky, as Paul learned this morning. Watch your fuel gauge. Return to the field with no less than a quarter tank. I'll have a crew there to pump fuel from dawn to dusk and another crew hauling fuel from Westbrook to keep the search planes supplied."

He spoke directly to Leif when he said, "Your uncle's plane is somewhere in our search area. I know it. Just as I know that we're going to find it—soon."

Suzanne followed Adam's gaze and found Leif sitting at a corner table with Jessica, Len, and Mr. Georges. Jessica, looking refreshed after her long trip, had changed to a magenta overblouse, belted loosely at the hips with a corded belt set off by a large brass buckle. She wore the same stunning gold jewelry as when she first arrived in Hastings.

"Any questions before I make afternoon assignments?"

"One comment, Adam," came a voice from a side booth. It was Rancher Johnson. "Sheriff Blake called in and asked me to relay his report. Before he went down the mountain this morning, he stopped by the miner's cabin, south of here. The miner did hear an aircraft overhead Thanksgiving Eve. He said it sounded like a truck coming up his washboard road. The miner also said that the plane was going to the south, coming from the north."

All eyes turned toward the aeronautical chart tacked on the bulletin board. *Rugged mountains, jagged peaks, sheer canyon walls. No place to land safely.*

"Two grids cover that broad area. Johnson, you take grid one and four. Your spotter will be my wife, Caroline. It's time to get her out of the kitchen."

Adam's moment of levity helped relax the tension building within the small band of searchers sobered under the weight of its responsibility. From now on, the countdown of life in sub-zero weather was measured in hours, minutes—if, there were still survivors clinging to earthtime.

"Paul, Kurt Schmidt, our resident editor, will spot for you. Grid two is your territory. Grid three, also, if there's time. Jake, you okay with Mr. Georges again?"

"Fine, Chief."

Suzanne perked up on that one.

Why not a switch on that team? Jake surely let Adam know his distaste for Mr. Georges by this time.

"Len, grids five and six. Doc Shaw knows that Devil's Gorge area. He'll spot for you.

"One more thing. We owe a debt of thanks to the Ladies' Guild for our wonderful lunch. Let me add that these same ladies have formed a telephone tree and will spend the afternoon calling most residents within a 30-mile radius to see if we can pinpoint the time, direction, and path of Stevens' flight over Hastings. If successful, we will be able to narrow our search area immensely."

He added as an afterthought, "Oh, yes,

Johnson will pass the word on the Indian reservation. He'll drive through it on his way back to his ranch this evening. Maybe one of the tribal members heard something."

Adam put his papers down, saying, "See you all here at 5 P.M. God bless your skyway."

As the group dispersed, Suzanne saw Adam motion to her. She made her way to the front of the room. "What may I do for you, 'Chief'?" Her eyes twinkled.

"Sounds like you're as well as you're going to be, Smarty."

She laughed softly. "I'm fine," she said, forgetting for a moment the building thunderheads of her day.

"Good. How about spotting this afternoon? Feel up to it, if Doctor Shaw gives his okay?"

"I'd love it! You know I would!"

"Then it's decided. I've got to run the fuel brigade this afternoon, so I've checked out a pilot in Eight-Kilo-Mike. You'll be flying in my plane. Leif Stevens will be your pilot."

Suzanne gasped.

A voice from behind her said, "I hope that meets with your approval, Miss Flynn."

Suzanne smiled. She knew when she turned around she would once again find Leif's dark eyes roguishly searching hers for an answer.

The answer was no secret to either of them.

Chapter Seven

"I see something! Go lower! Go lower!" Suzanne cried excitedly into the mike mounted on her headset.

"Where?" asked Leif.

"Below my window at 2 o'clock."

Leif dipped the right wing and leaned across in front of Suzanne in order to look out her window. The intoxicating aroma of his after-shave lotion sent her head spinning.

"I believe what you're seeing is our own shadow splashed on that ribbon of rocks above the river," he said from behind aviator-styled dark glasses.

"No, Leif. I've been watching our shadow move with us. This is something different. We're past it now."

"I'll make a one-eighty and come back across the same area. Tell me as soon as you see it."

Suzanne braced herself as Leif banked sharply, sending the horizon into a new axis with her equilibrium. She relaxed, allowing herself to absorb the vivid colors kaleido-scoping in the galaxy below.

"The Turbo 210 is a terrific machine. I have one like it. Unfortunately, it's a little fast for a search plane, so keep a close watch."

"There. See? The sun's reflecting off something metal."

Leif lowered the nose of the Cessna. She watched the altimeter as the plane descended, then leveled off.

"Look, Suzanne, it's an old tin shed, prob-ably a pumping station for the aqueduct."

Suzanne sighed disappointedly and straight-ened the collar on the royal-blue, wool Eisenhower jacket she was wearing. The matching pants and accenting hand-printed blouse, combined to give her a total look that was as electric as the tone of her clear, blue eyes.

All the while they were flying at low alti-tudes, Suzanne kept her head turned toward the window, her eyes studying the landscape below, painted this time of year almost solely in a snowy whitewash, trimmed in rock browns and grays with occasional touches of ice blue.

Leif's attention was on his flying—as low as safely possible among the jutting peaks with their unpredictable, perilous updrafts and downdrafts—currents, that without an instant's warning could snare their light plane and fling it into a death spin.

Finally, they soared out over the high desert to make a 90-degree turn, travel for three miles, then make a second 90-degree turn for another pass over their assigned grid area. It was only during these "end runs" that they could safely exchange a few words.

With the hum of the engine of the high-winged plane in the background, Leif asked, "What brought you to Hastings?"

"A job offer and the desire to get away from city smog and congestion. I had just graduated from the University of Southern California and was anxious to get out on my own, too," she replied, still keeping her vigil of the terrain far below—just in case.

Then she added thoughtfully, "The High Sierras are a collection of God's richest handiwork."

"Perhaps it's because most of it is so close to heaven, sort of a geological dessert topping," Leif commented lightly, nosing the plane up 100 feet. "Where's your family?"

"In the Los Angeles area. My father is a minister, my mother a school teacher. I have two younger brothers. One wants to be an astronaut, the other a fireman. Matt's family background is basically the same as mine."

"Matt. Yes, Matt—the man of the moment in your life."

Suzanne, surprised by Leif's sudden curt tone of voice, glanced at him long enough to notice a rigidness in his jawline. She quickly turned back to her assignment.

"When's the wedding?" Leif made a vain attempt to soften his tone.

She was trying to think of a response other than "None of your business" when Leif exclaimed, "Something's moving—down to my left, near that clump of sagebrush, about 9 o'clock. See it?"

Suzanne unbuckled her seat belt, put her knees on the seat so she could look past the pilot and down to the place he pinpointed. Just then, the plane dipped sharply to the left, throwing Suzanne off balance and sending her crashing against Leif's shoulder.

"Only stray cattle," Leif noted, as Suzanne landed awkwardly against him.

She squealed and struggled but could not right herself until Leif leveled the craft. He laughed as he quickly trimmed the plane, then pushed crimson-faced Suzanne out of his way.

"Ouch!" A strand of my hair is caught in your jacket zipper," she exclaimed.

"Guess we'll have to cut your hair off," Leif teased, his eyes still on his flying.

"Not on your life, Mr. Stevens. It's my winter coat."

"Then you'll have to stay attached to me forever," he said seriously, lowering his head and kissing her on the tip of her nose.

Suzanne felt her whole body tingle as Leif looked questioningly into her eyes for just an instant. It was long enough for her to sense that he was as overwhelmed by what was happening as she was.

Suzanne broke the magnetism of the moment with her reply. "It would crowd your life a little, don't you think?" Then she gave one good yank, freeing the strand of hair and the bond that held them close.

Leif adjusted the controls slightly and answered wistfully, "You're right, of course."

They coursed through the sky in silence for a few minutes, back toward the rugged mountains. As Suzanne's eyes searched for the downed plane, her mind was scrambling to sort out the new feelings surging through her body.

It was just a quick kiss. It happened on the spur of the moment. It didn't mean anything— to either one of us. After all, Leif's in love with Jessica. He's asked her to spend the rest of her life with him!

Then, suddenly, Suzanne felt angry. *I wouldn't want the man I'm going to marry going around kissing other women—even if thrown together for a moment, accidentally.*

At the next end turn she asked, "When are you and Jessica getting married?" She'd lay a little guilt on the brazen bachelor sitting next to her. She could almost feel Leif squirm in the left seat as he evaded a direct answer.

"We have some things to work out. Things I didn't believe were important when we made a lifelong commitment to one another six months ago."

Sounds like a reluctant groom's counterpart line to "My wife doesn't understand me," mused Suzanne. *Next he'll tell me that he needs a friend like me to talk to—someone who understands him. He'll suggest that we "talk" sometime when no one else knows about it— "We wouldn't want people to get the wrong idea, would we?"*

"You see, Suzanne, Jessica and I have different values on some issues."

Here comes the "Feel sorry for me" chorus.

"Part of our attraction to one another is that we both believe that one accepts a person the way he or she is, that trying to change a person once you're married is down payment on a divorce decree."

No sympathy from me, fellow. "Looks like you understand each other pretty well."

"Yes," he sighed. "Jessica's easy to talk to. Not like some women who second-guess everything or clam up. It was very easy for us to become friends, to appreciate the other's strengths."

"So. . .?"

Leif smiled. "That's one of the things I like about you, friend. You're anxious to get to the root of the matter, without dancing around the mulberry bush. You may be the one person who can help me with Jessica. She. . ."

"My father calls it impatience. I call it honesty. Jessica is your problem. Not mine. The root here is—I do not want to be your 'friend.' "

Silence again. The mountains were back. Leif descended cautiously between two ridges. She studied the terrain outside her window carefully. Leif was too busy flying the plane to take more than a quick sidelong glance occasionally out his side window. *Every plane needs two spotters. A second one in the back seat behind the pilot. Otherwise, we need to cover this exact air space again, coming from the opposite direction.*

All of a sudden Suzanne's stomach did a flip-flop and she was looking up at the sky above instead of the ground below. The right wing shot over her head. The tiny plane was tipping over! Leif was going to kill them both!

"Hang on!" Leif called out. "We're banking sharply and spiraling down."

And hang on Suzanne did! Down they spun on a three-dimensional serpentine ride, away from a towering wall of granite on their right. When Leif leveled off they were 500 feet above the canyon floor racing a tiny tributary toward the setting sun.

"Sorry," Leif apologized. "The unexpected sometimes throws a pilot into a tailspin."

"I thought you were trying to compete with Bob Hoover," Suzanne quipped nervously.

"Bob Hoover? How do you know him?" Leif brought the nose up and the plane rose gracefully out of the canyon.

Suzanne's eyes busily returned to scanning while she salved Leif's curiosity. "I watched him perform his daring aerial skills in the Shrike Commander at the Reno Air Races last fall."

"Oh, yes. . .it was his twentieth year of precision demonstrations at Reno—also the twentieth anniversary of the Reno National Championship Air Races—the premier air racing and air show event in the world. It's the only place on earth where 'big iron,' the Unlimiteds, fly and the only place where you can see four other classes of airplanes compete —AT / 6, Formula, Sport Biplane, and Racing Biplane."

Suzanne could not help but ask, "How is it you know so much about the Reno Air Races?"

"Airplanes are not only my vocation,

they're my avocation. Spaceships are my job, airplanes my hobby. While in college, I was fortunate enough to work on a pit crew for one of the Unlimiteds. I haven't been the same since. Someday, I'd like to restore old planes, own a racing team or . . . who knows? It all takes money and space."

"Look straight ahead. What's that?" Suzanne questioned.

"A miner's cabin with a tin roof, I'd guess. We'll take a closer look."

"I think my eyes are playing tricks on me. Rocks and shadows are beginning to look like wings of a plane," Suzanne commented, rubbing her right temple with her fingertips.

"We want so much to find that plane . . . before it's too late." Leif's words were weighted with discouragement.

Again, the droning silence. A gray curtain fell across the sun, casting long shadows where none had been before. Suzanne's eyes began to water with weariness. At last, the final lap ahead!

"All the talk has been about the search, the plane, the men. We haven't had time to talk about the people we're looking for. What's your uncle like?"

"A bull of a man in size. A teddy bear in personality. He grew up in these parts, but when my father was killed, something died within him, too, he always said, in explaining why he sold off most of the cattle and moved to family land in California. "Still Uncle Carl comes up here a couple times a year to check on the ranch and to hunt."

"Your uncle and Bill Daniels—they weren't on a hunting trip, were they?"

"No."

"I heard they were going to Oregon to Bill Daniels' ranch."

"Yes, Bill had to sign a couple property deeds. I figure the deadline caused them to use poor judgment to try to beat the storm to Oregon. Once they realized they were in trouble, I suspect they either decided to turn back or to detour to the Stevens Ranch to wait out the storm. Either they didn't find the ranch or, if they did, the landing strip was not plowed clear of snow. Remember, the caretaker was not expecting them, especially during the winter's first blizzard."

"Say you're right so far. If you were them, what would you do next?"

"Head east, away from the storm area. It's what any pilot would do."

Suzanne pushed on excitedly. "Can't we call weather and find out exactly what area the storm covered about 8 P.M. the night before Thanksgiving?"

"Good idea. Only there are some variables. Neither Daniels nor my uncle checked with weather, at all, around that time. Evidently they thought they knew which way to go— which could be any direction. Their radio or other instruments may have fouled up as well."

"And no one knows how long they went around in circles over Hastings or how much fuel they used since Stockton," she reflected softly.

Leif reached over and patted her on the shoulder. She pretended to bristle.

Both were silent for a moment. Then Leif began haltingly. "No one... no one has really talked about the most likely culprit in this nightmare."

"What do you mean?"

"Ice."

"Ice?"

"They were in a freezing blizzard. Obviously, there was moisture in the air. It doesn't take long for ice to form on the wings. A wing is nothing more than an air foil. When the air foil shape is altered the plane loses lift."

"What happens then?"

"The plane loses altitude—fast. If the plane descends below the freezing level, the ice begins to melt. Hopefully, the pilot has a chance to regain control before crashing."

"Wouldn't it be impossible to fly low enough in a blizzard in the High Sierra to stay under the freezing level..."

"Without smacking into a mountain? Affirmative, in this case."

"How about flying up, to get above the

freezing level, by getting on top of the storm?"

"I'll take you on my team anytime. You don't give up easily, do you?"

"There are two lives at stake. . ."

"I know. How well I know. Your enthusiasm is refreshing, but the freezing level of the monstrous storm in question rose well above the ceiling of Daniels' plane's flying capability. Even so, they'd have iced-up during the long climb."

For the first time, Suzanne fully realized the odds of the mission. As they flew the last lap in fast-fading light, that reoccurring heaviness in her heart returned, as did the memory of the frantic sound of the floundering plane overhead on Thanksgiving Eve. It was a cry for help she'd never forget. *The plane was so close then—so close and yet so far from safety. Both men were alive and warm—just a few feet above us in the storm. Oh, Lord, lead us to them soon.*

The sunset was behind them when Leif pulled the nose up for the final time and set the course for Hastings. Suzanne had an idea.

"Let's get more planes in the air, cover the area more quickly. Is that a possibility?"

"The CAP is on its own. I have no control over how many planes they commit to the search, where they search, or how long they continue to chalk up hours on this mission," replied Leif, as if there had been no break in their conversation.

"The search team in Hastings is strictly a private venture—although the CAP cooperates with us. We have to come up with the financing. For instance, it costs $70 minimum an hour to fly the plane we're in right now. The good people of Hastings have bitten the bullet so far. I can't ask for one hour more, nor could I accept it. I've called home and talked to both Bill, Daniels' business partner and the principles in my uncle's firm. I should know by tomorrow morning, Saturday, how many more planes, pilots, spotters, and cash we have to work with."

Leif sighed tiredly and continued. "There are only a couple of things I'm sure of. One, my uncle's plane landed somewhere within the Hastings search area. If he survived the crash, he's still alive because he's a mountain man. He knows how to work with this weather. I won't stop searching until I find him—he knows that, too."

"What's the other thing you know for sure?" Suzanne asked, noticing that Leif was deliberately keeping his eyes from her.

"I know that I could have used a good friend."

Chapter Eight

"I see you got my message," Matt said, helping Suzanne down the icy steps in front of the Woloskis' home.

"It was on my pillow when I came home last night after the briefing. Bessie pinned it there before she and Ned drove over to her sister's for an early dinner. Beside the note was a chocolate mint. I tell you, those two are something special!"

"So are you," Matt whispered, pulling her close as they walked to his car.

"Thank you, Matt. I don't know what I'd do without you."

"Keep thinking that, will you?" he said, opening the car door for her. They were due at Adam's Rib for a Saturday morning 7 A.M. briefing.

She was glad that he shut the door then, and sorry that she'd fed him a line to build his hopes on.

"Did you find Holly yesterday afternoon?" was her first question as Matt opened his door and settled himself behind the wheel.

"Me first," insisted Matt. "This is important. Did you talk with Ned about his trip to the county seat?"

"I haven't had a chance. They came in late last night and were still asleep—or at least still in their bedroom, when you came for me a minute ago."

"Ned's an early riser. Do you think he's avoiding . . . ?"

"Yes, Matt, I do. There's nothing I can do to make him tell me, if he doesn't want to . . ."

"It's Holly who is our primary concern," Matt said. "We have to deal with her situation today. We can't procrastinate any longer, waiting on Ned and his 'maybe' involvement."

Suzanne sensed an urgency in Matt's voice. "Matt, it's not that I want to avoid the issue, I just don't know how to approach it. It takes more nerve than I've had to interfere in a student's family life. But, the time has come, I agree. I'll go out to the motel this morning and talk with her. I promise."

"By 'we' I meant us. I think I should come with you."

"Her teacher and her pastor showing up together—unannounced? That would frighten Holly. I know it would have me when I was thirteen." Still, she pondered Matt's suggestion a long moment before she replied decidedly, "I'll go alone. Besides, you're really not supposed to know anything about the money or her possible illness."

After another moment of reflection her resolve wavered. "It is true, though, I've made matters worse at every opportunity . . . maybe I'm not the one for the job."

"Now—don't *you* be so hard on yourself. 'All things work together for good to them that love God.' "

"I know. Romans 8:28—one of the 100 verses I memorized in the third grade. That's how I earned my first 'very own' Bible."

"What I'm trying to say, Suzanne, is that what may appear as a bunch of botch-ups to you—is really part of God's perfect timing. Remember, everything is in His time. Trust Him. You'll know exactly how to handle the situation when you get there."

Matt personalized his point by adding, "I sense your same frustration. You'll understand what I mean in a minute as I also answer your question. Yes—yes, I did find Holly. She was at Penny's when I called there requesting a meeting of the junior high / high school group at 3 P.M. at search headquarters."

"What was your excuse for the meeting?"

"No excuse—a reason. Mr. King brought in his mobile radio unit for the search team to use as ground control. By setting the frequency at 122.75, the ground control operator, in this case one of our older teens, will be able to keep in touch with the search planes, as they can each other. Another safety precaution."

"That's a big responsibility for a 17-year-old," Suzanne said.

"Do you know the average age of the pilots who saved America from Hitler in World War II? Anyway, there will always be an adult in the headquarters. It just frees the supervisor for other tasks while Kevin, Keith, or Louie monitor the radio."

"Did Penny and Holly show for the meeting? And what did you have in mind for the junior high kids to do?"

"Yes, to answer your first question. The girls were both there. As you said, Holly looked beat. I welcomed her. And as I thanked her for coming, Suzanne, I looked into her eyes—and found no one home." Matt's voice faltered. He swallowed hard before finishing his remarks. "She wasn't there 10 minutes before her father came by to pick her up. I was shocked to see him so soon. In retrospect, I should have dropped everything the moment I looked into her eyes. I should have taken her aside then. My schedule with the group could have waited."

"But you didn't know that your minutes with Holly were numbered—that she was about to slip from grasp—again."

"Exactly. I have to believe that things are being done according to God's will—including now, our commitment to find that child and discover what's going on in her life!"

No wonder the urgency in his voice. Holly is exhausted. She's fighting something—physically, emotionally, and perhaps spiritually.

Lord, help me find her in time. Help me find her before she gives up. She needs me, I know it!

Suzanne did not press an answer to her second question. It just didn't seem important anymore. They drove in silence the remaining couple of minutes until they reached the restaurant.

Matt swung into the unusually crowded parking lot. Several out-of-town four-wheel-drive pickups, pulling snowmobile trailers had commandeered two parking spots each.

"Let's go see what's going on," Matt said with concern, nodding to the group of men gathered in front of one of the trucks. Leif was talking to one of them.

Matt climbed out of the car and was striding purposefully toward the group when Suzanne noticed the common denominator of the recent arrivals.

The seven or eight of them were dressed identically—in red, cold-weather jump suits, set off with long, black scarves slung rakishly around their necks and over their shoulders. A stocky member of the group, with a flushed face and beer-belly, carried a matching red helmet.

Suzanne zipped up her ski jacket. Under it she wore a pink, cotton turtleneck, covered with a crew-neck sweater. It was navy blue, the same color as her wool slacks. Knitted into the sweater were tiny flowers in pink and green. Suzanne liked the feminine, petite feeling the outfit gave her. She brushed her hand against her hair, flipping the long, side strands behind her shoulders, exposing hand-carved, gold-loop earrings, a birthday gift from her parents. Then she grabbed her soft, eel-skin shoulder bag and followed after Matt.

She walked up as one of the men was saying, "As I told your friend here, Pastor, we heard about the lost plane on the radio. We're the Snow-Knights. We spend our winter weekends offering a search-and-rescue service. With our snowmobiles, we are able to attack remote areas inaccessible to traditional rescue teams."

Leif broke in. "And I told you, we haven't

a clue as to where the crash site is located. It could be in Idaho!"

"We're here. Why don't we spend the day searching the Hastings area? Your search headquarters are here. It must be the most logical. . ."

"How much?" Leif interrupted impatiently.

"You got a price tag on your uncle's life, man?"

"Why you. . ." Leif started toward the cocky-mouthed leader.

Matt quickly stepped between the two. The snowmobiler retreated a couple of paces, put his hands on his hips, and sneered.

Matt looked to Leif apprehensively. Leif's flashing eyes mellowed, the twitch at his jawline softened. Matt stepped back. For the first time, Leif noticed Suzanne's presence.

"Jessica's inside. Please go and keep her company. We'll be in shortly."

Suzanne did as she was told without a word. As soon as she was inside, she hurried to the nearest window and looked out, keeping herself hidden from view by the ruffled, yellow chintz curtain draped at the window's edge.

"Playing hide-and-seek?"

"Oh! You startled me, Mr. Georges." Suzanne caught her breath and explained the situation outside, which seemed quite calm now.

Then she smiled and placed her hand on the

70-year-old retired grocer's arm. "May I join you for a cup of hot chocolate?"

"Of. . .of course," he responded uncertainly. "Jake and I are just finishing up at that booth by the door." He gestured to his plaid-shirted search partner, who nodded approvingly. Then Mr. Georges stepped aside, allowing Suzanne to lead the way.

It's hard to believe my eyes. First, Mr. McCafferty accuses Mr. Georges of heresy and then wants to ask him to leave the church. Then he fights like a trapped bear when Georges is assigned as his search partner. After one ride together, McCafferty quits complaining. Now, to top it off, he's met this slightly eccentric gentleman for breakfast!

Suzanne slipped into the booth and greeted Jake.

"How's Robert feeling? Mumps are tough to have at this age."

"He's raring to get back to school Monday. He won't admit it, but I think he misses U.S. history the most."

"Or Melissa Shaw, who sits in front of him," she grinned.

Mr. Georges pulled up a chair and sat down at the end of the table. Suzanne handed him a freshly filled cup of coffee. As he reached out and took it, his hand shook so that some of the coffee spilled on the table.

She was aware that Jake pretended not to notice.

Suzanne rushed to cover. "The reason I asked to join you, Mr. Georges, is to express my appreciation to you for pulling me from the burning church the other evening. My thanks are long overdue—nevertheless, deeply and sincerely felt. I'm at a loss as to know how I can ever repay you and Ned for saving my life."

"God didn't want you punished. It wasn't meant for you to die."

"He pulled you from the church, saved your life?"

Suzanne could not understand Jake's surprise. "Yes...He and Ned, although Mr. Georges dragged me half out of the vestibule before Ned arrived."

Jake sat back and shook his head.

Puzzled though she was by Jake's disbelief, she felt compelled to speak to Mr. Georges' last remark.

"God doesn't punish Christians. All of our sins—past, present, and future—have been paid for. Christ took all our punishment on the cross. God *does* discipline His own, in order that we may be drawn into a closer relationship with Him. We're reminded of that truth in many of the Bible stories. God punished, even destroyed, nations for their sins. His own Israel, He only disciplined—to bring them to repentance. He's promised never to destroy His people—the nation of believers. There will always be a remnant."

Mr. Georges retorted bitterly, "God may not punish His own, but my own church brothers, in the name of Christ, have accused me falsely, and without a trial have judged me. They're pressing to punish me—cutting me off from my brothers and sisters."

Then his voice shook angrily as he spat out the next words. "Wait until I find out which of my cowardly Christian brothers has secretly taken up the banner against me!"

Jake McCafferty lowered his head, burying it in his hands, but not before she glimpsed the pained look that crossed his face and filled his eyes.

"I know there has been some gossip about your trip—your 'faith healing'. . . "

"Gossip! A sin no less serious in God's eyes than murder!"

Jake's face grew red around the edges of his gnarled hands.

"What I am guilty of is telling Martha Pettijohn about my trip before I left, as I asked her to feed my cat. Upon my return, I excitedly told her of its success. I knew she'd spread it faster than hot butter. I asked myself, what difference does it make? Thomas and I both praise God for the healing."

Suzanne, totally deflated, stared at both men, sensing the crosscurrents of pain and bitterness they unknowingly shared for and against one another.

"May I take your order?"

Suzanne looked up. "Oh . . . yes. Except that I'm not at my own table and these gentlemen are finished."

"We're leaving," Jake said. "Adam's given us our orders. Half a day is all we get. Storm's coming in."

The two left. Suzanne stood and hastily scanned the room for Jessica, whom she'd forgotten about, when she saw a tall, model-like figure coming from the direction of the ladies' room. Jessica appeared relaxed, dressed comfortably in powder-blue slacks and a cream-colored cable-knit sweater with a rolled collar.

Thank You, Lord, for Your perfect timing, she prayed silently as the two walked to a window table and sat down. Suzanne glanced outside to the parking lot. The snowmen were getting into their vehicles. Matt and Leif were walking toward the front door.

"Leif looks good as a cowboy, don't you think?" Suzanne asked as a conversation starter. "His clothes seem to fit today. I confess, his Levis and fleece-lined, suede jacket look more like Hastings General Store open stock than anything you could buy in San Francisco."

"You have a sensitive eye for handsome men, I see." Jessica's eyes narrowed as she seemed to appraise Suzanne for the first time.

Jessica sighed heavily and continued on cryptically. "The truth is, those *are* Hastings' best 'duds'—as the shopkeeper called them, when he opened the store for us last evening. Leif refused to wear the casual attire I picked out for him at his apartment."

Suzanne cringed at the thought of Jessica intimate enough with Leif to fold and pack his personal belongings, until Jessica added, "Leif said last night that he wants more Levis and more of Hastings. Can you imagine, after all these years, he wants to drive out and look over his ranch when this is all over!" She pulled out a cigarette and dropped the package disgustedly on the table.

The smile that crossed Suzanne's face began in her heart.

"The only way we'll be at the opera in San Francisco tonight is to take a break from this place for the weekend," clipped Jessica.

Suzanne did not offer the news that a storm front was moving in and that any leaving would have to be done by noon today. However, the secret was out a minute later when they were joined by Leif, Matt, Len, and Paul.

Leif sat down across from Suzanne, next to Jessica. He directed his comments to both ladies when he said, "Paul will be leaving later this morning, long before the storm hits. He and the plane are needed back at corporate headquarters. Even though we were not able to use his low-wing plane for searching, we are grateful that he was here to take the controls of Rancher Dunlap's 182."

Paul tossed in, "Dunlap's broken arm didn't keep him from spotting, though."

"So many here have given us so much..." Leif's voice trailed off for a moment. Then, back on track, he added, "Len's Cardinal has developed alternator trouble. He's headed back to San Francisco this morning, also. Frankly, that's where his talents can best be used this weekend."

"What can he do at home that you couldn't do there this weekend?" Jessica asked petulantly.

"He's going to call on my aunt and on Bill Daniels' wife. Although family is with both of them, they deserve to hear firsthand what efforts are being made to rescue their husbands. I can only imagine their grief, their frustration..."

"I'm also going to find out why more searchers haven't arrived from among Daniels' business partners. There's also the subject of money..." Len interjected.

Leif spoke up. "There isn't much cash in the family trust fund. We'd have to petition the court. That takes time—time we don't have. Only $1000 has been pledged toward search costs by friends of the men. Len believes he can generate more assistance—personally, than over a long-distance telephone line. We can't lean on Hastings' bottomless hospitality any longer. We've got to start paying our own way!" Leif stated emphatically.

"Those fellows out front were ready to relieve you of that $1000 for one day's ride," Matt interjected.

"I didn't know whether to fight them or to do business with them until my brain connected with the black logo painted on the front of their helmets. I wanted nothing to do with them either way after that."

Just then, Adam arrived with his clipboard and pulled up a chair. Leif acknowledged him, then continued.

"Adam, here, has suggested that we take our first dollars and hire a local bush pilot, who could fly in and out of the canyons in a slow-flying plane. Bush pilots are used in the area to locate stray cattle as well as wounded game that make a desperate run for the mountains. Bush pilots have a high degree of confidence and are not afraid to take chances."

"I suggest Ted Eilertson," said Adam. "He lives only 15 miles south of here. He's one of the best—and available."

"Hire him," Leif said. "We'll use him as long as the money holds out. I feel awful, Adam, paying him, when we should first pay you and the other ranchers who've given us many free hours."

"And we'll give more free hours." Adam spoke with finality. "So let's get down to business." He referred to the notes on his clipboard. "First off, Idaho has called off its search team. Oregon reports a downed plane of its own. It will concentrate on that search in the central part of the state. Nevada will conclude its participation in our search today with a five-plane search northeast of us. I'd say we're on our own. So let's get with it. All of the other teams are on their way to the airport."

Adam started to stand. "Wait," Jessica said. She turned to Leif and asked, "What about my suggestion? It hasn't been discussed as a possibility."

Adam sat down on the edge of his chair. Leif scowled but had no choice but to present Jessica's plan.

"Jessica wants to hire a clairvoyant."

"Good idea!" agreed Len. "Let's hire the one that solves all those murders for the police."

Jessica brightened at Len's enthusiastic support.

"Once the word is out, you'll be deluged with quacks—all who want to be paid in advance for their guesses," offered Adam.

"Clairvoyants are not prophets, they're of the devil," advised Matt.

Leif shrugged his shoulders. "I rest my case, Jessica."

The men stood up. "Let's go, Jessica. Will you be our second spotter this morning, Suzanne?" Leif asked.

"Sorry, I've got a professional matter that needs attending to. I've put it off as long as I can." Suzanne hoped no one else could read the disappointment registered in Leif's eyes.

"I'll go with you, Leif," offered Matt. "My painting crew told me to stay away from the church this morning. They saw what I did to the parsonage."

Matt's remark drew chuckles. In the commotion of pushing in chairs and gathering coats, Suzanne asked Leif, "What was the logo on the Snow Knights' helmets? I'm curious to know what made you consider them less than worthy."

"A five-pointed star pointed downward—the sign of Satan."

"You're...you're a Christian?" her voice trembled.

His dark eyes commanded hers. When he spoke it was with certainty.

"Yes, I am," he replied.

Chapter Nine

"Good morning, Mrs. McArthur. I've come to see Holly." Suzanne looked straight into the middle-aged woman's heavy-lidded eyes. There would be no mistaking the seriousness of her intent.

Helen McArthur, a large woman with freckles everywhere her skin showed, and red, frizzy hair that was definitely not her own color, turned away from the chipped Formica reception counter and slowly shuffled in leather slippers toward the room in the rear. Her sweat suit had seen healthier days.

Suzanne could not see beyond the garish, fern-print curtain, but she could hear the T.V. blaring out an "I Love Lucy" rerun. A mixture of stale smoke and cooking grease hung in the air.

Once the woman was behind the curtain, Suzanne overheard conversation between the husband and wife, although she could not discern any of the words.

A minute later, the tired-looking curtain was flung aside and Mrs. McArthur reappeared.

"Why?"

"Why what?" asked Suzanne straight-faced.

The woman hadn't expected the soft-spoken schoolteacher to play her game.

"Why do you want to see Holly?"

"It's more than that. I *need* to see her. If she's asleep, I'll wait here until she awakens."

The woman's face reddened. She turned and repeated the shuffling process until she passed through the well-worn curtain one more time.

It didn't take long for Mr. McArthur to come storming through the opening. His hair was uncombed, his plaid shirt unbuttoned, exposing a well-dinnered undershirt. The shredded cuffs of his underslung work pants dragged on the floor at his heel line. Suzanne would not allow herself to be intimidated by the man's clenched fists and reddened face. Before he reached his side of the counter, she smelled the stench of cheap wine.

"Good day, Miss Flynn. Nice of you to drop in. However, it will be impossible for you to see Holly today. She's not here."

"Where is she?" There wasn't a hint of softness in Suzanne's voice.

"She's spending the holiday weekend with her cousins down the hill. I'm sure Monday will be soon enough for you to see her, won't it?"

Is he so drunk that he's forgotten that Holly was in town only yesterday?"

"When did she go down the hill?"

"For Thanksgiving. We were too busy to set a holiday table, so she. . ."

"My family has its Thanksgiving dinner on Sunday. My husband's a little confused. Mr. McArthur took her down last night."

Mrs. McArthur's recovery was too little and too late. Suzanne didn't like being made a fool of. She liked even less the thought of Holly in serious trouble—and the cause of that trouble was standing in a stupor on the other side of the counter!

"You're wrong, Mr. McArthur. Monday will be far too late! I intend to see her today. I would appreciate it if you would give me the address where she can be reached. I'd like to be on my way before the storm hits."

Mrs. McArthur looked nervously at her husband. He stared at Suzanne, appearing to weigh Suzanne's ability to bluff.

"Don't know the address. We just go there. We don't read road signs."

"Then, Mr. McArthur, I'll find the address for myself. Her nearest relative, other than her parents, is listed on her school application form. Good day to you both." Suzanne turned and hurried from the room.

She only began to shake once she was outside and tried to descend the narrow, icy stairs to the parking lot below the aging motel. The buildings hadn't been touched with a paintbrush since the McArthurs bought it two years ago.

She reached the car and fumbled in her purse for her keys. *Normal parents would have been delighted to have their daughter's teacher call. Not defensive, suspicious, and almost panicked by my need to find Holly. Holly is in danger. I know it!*

She slipped the key into the lock. Once in the car, she started the engine, then reached out to pull the door shut.

"Just a minute, Miss Flynn. We're not finished, you and I!"

Suzanne looked up into the angry, contorted face of Holly's father. His claw-like hand gripped the open door.

"What Holly does outside school hours is none of your affair. She's keeping up her grades, that I know. I'm telling you only once. Keep away from her. You talk to her about anything but schoolwork and I swear, you'll pay for it—painfully! And so will Holly!"

Suzanne's eyes narrowed. She was in full control as she said clearly, evenly, "I believe, Mr. McArthur, before I go find Holly, I'll pay a visit to the sheriff!"

She anticipated McArthur's lunge almost before it happened. The instant he let go of the door frame, Suzanne tromped on the gas pedal. The car lurched forward and McArthur fell headlong into the slushy snow. Suzanne reached out, grabbed the door, and pulled it shut without lifting her foot from the accelerator. She drove as fast as she dared out the potholed driveway. Suzanne paused at the main highway only long enough to check for oncoming traffic and to glance into the rearview mirror.

McArthur had reached his mud-covered pickup and was coming after her!

Chapter Ten

Panic washed over her. *Which way shall I go? Left to the highway? Maybe I'll spot a highway patrolman. . . what if I don't? There's a service station five miles south. I can get help there. . . but they're not always open. To the right? How fast can I drive the winding road back to town? And I may not see a car the whole way. How would I signal one to stop if I did meet a car?*

She glanced behind her. McArthur was closing the gap between them! She made her decision and turned through the slush onto the paved road. She headed toward town. *I pray I've made the right choice!*

She pressed the accelerator and watched the needle move up the speedometer. The main road was dry on the straightaways, but she slowed on tree-shaded curves, where melting snow ran from the high side then froze in a slick sheet across both lanes.

If I spin out he'll catch me for sure! Suzanne took her eyes from the road only an instant to track her pursuer. *Dear Lord! He's only a few yards behind me! His shoulders are hunched. He's determined to catch me and. . .*

Sharp curve ahead. Suzanne looked back at the road just in time to notice a slow-moving farm tractor, pulling a load of firewood, disappear around the bend. She was in the curve. Too late to stop!

Suzanne jerked the steering wheel to the left, stomped on the gas pedal and flipped on her headlights. She sped by the startled ranch hand in the oncoming lane of the blind curve. Once past the tractor, she swung back into her own lane without decreasing speed. *Thank You, God—not for having a car coming at me and for the straightaway ahead!*

She glanced in her rearview mirror. McArthur was temporarily stuck behind the tractor—but only until they came out of the curve. Suzanne pressed harder on the accelerator, praying there wasn't a patch of black ice in her path.

Hairpin turn ahead—a 1000-foot fall on the right. Suzanne tested her brakes gently, then more firmly as the curve loomed closer. If McArthur caught her now, so be it. This was "Death's Turn." But it wasn't going to be hers.

Another curve, another long, straight stretch. McArthur gained steadily. Suzanne's knuckles blanched white. Perspiration glistened on her forehead. Her mouth was dry. She pressed the accelerator to the floor.

Suddenly—a cracking jolt! McArthur bumped her from the rear! It was a square hit. McArthur moved to straddle the white line. He was coming at her again. This time he was aiming for the left side of her bumper. *He wants to send me flying out of control and over the edge!*

Suzanne started weaving her tiny car back and forth across the two lanes. It slowed her down, but what difference did it make? He had caught her. It was important now to keep out of his way.

Then it happened. A snowflake hit the windshield. Then another. Thirty seconds later the windshield wipers could hardly sweep them out of her way. Hallelujah! God had sent hailstones from heaven to protect Joshua from the enemy. Why not a snow screen for Suzanne?

Suddenly, McArthur pulled alongside, motioning her to pull over. Suzanne set her jaw and stared straight ahead. She grasped the wheel tighter, waiting for him to sideswipe her car, to send it crashing over the low metal railing and the precipice beyond.

Instead, McArthur sped ahead. *What's he up to?* Then she knew! He was racing ahead to gain time to stop, turn broadside, and block the road!

She slowed to avoid the inevitable confrontation awaiting her around the next bend. Then—the snow flurry stopped as suddenly as it had begun and Suzanne instantly recognized where she was.

Yes, there on the left, in the distance—the airport hangars. And just ahead, nearly indistinguishable, the cutoff to the airfield. She was certain McArthur hadn't seen it because of the snow flurry. She would have passed it then, too.

She turned onto the road, carefully. She wished there was some way to hide her fresh tracks. She'd like that madman to think she had vanished into space.

Then she gasped. *What have I done? This is a dead-end road! There won't be anyone out here in a snowstorm!*

It was too late. She saw McArthur's lights coming back down the road, retracing his route to find her. If she could see his lights, he could see hers.

Suzanne leaned forward, peering ahead in desperation, straining her eyes through the grayness. Was it panic or snow blindness that conjured up a vehicle parked near Adam's hangar? Lights flashed in her rearview mirror. McArthur had turned down the airport road and was in hot pursuit!

It *was* a vehicle. It was Adam's four-wheel-drive! That meant Leif was still up in the sky searching—in the snowstorm! A fresh wave of panic drenched her as images of another floundering plane, crying desperately for help, circled above—only to disappear! *Leif, not you, too!*

Lights bounced in her mirror. *He's getting closer.* A heavy snow started to fall again. She floored the gas pedal and surged ahead. Thirty feet later she hit a dip, lost traction, and spun sideways into a snowbank.

Suzanne threw the gear into reverse. The wheels spun. She was hopelessly stuck. She switched off the engine, opened the door, and jumped into the snow. A second later she was running down the road toward the hangar— toward Adam's vehicle. *I pray Leif left the keys in the ignition—*

She glanced over her shoulder. The heavily falling snow curtained everything behind her except a pair of snow-filtered headlights dimly piercing the grayness.

He's at my car. He'll run me down in a minute if I stay on the road.

Suzanne hurriedly climbed the icy drift at the edge of the road and trudged across the field as fast as she could maneuver through the deep snow.

There was no wind. In the eerie silence she heard McArthur slam her car door. She heard the noise of metal on metal as he rousted around in the toolbox in the back of his pickup.

Is he going to pull my car out of the snowbank? He can have it! I'm not going back!

Suzanne stumbled and fell. She got up quickly and brushed the wet snow from her arms as she ran on. Her lungs ached from the unrelenting bombardment of freezing air. Then she heard it—the cocking of a rifle. She stopped, stunned.

She was running again, before he fired the first shot. She couldn't tell how close it came; she just knew he had fired in the right direction—and that frightened her!

Suzanne fell again. This time she kept falling—and falling. She was trapped, chest high, in a snowdrift. The harder she tried to climb out the deeper she sank.

"I know you're out there in the field, Teacher. I'm coming out to get you. I'm gonna pick you off like a wimpering pigeon." McArthur fired a second shot.

Suzanne closed her eyes. She was trapped and alone. There was no way to escape, no way to reach Adam's truck. She was getting cold, too cold. To move an inch was to sink another foot.

"Where are you, Teacher?" A third shot.

She was slipping, she knew it. There was peace in her heart when her mind called upon the prayer of her childhood.

Unto Thy hands I commend myself, my body and soul, and all things. Let Thy Holy Spirit be with me that this wicked foe may have no power over me. In Jesus' name...

"Suzanne... Suzanne..."

So this is what it's like to die and go to heaven. I hear the Lord calling. I'm here. I'm ready.

"Suzanne... Suzanne... answer me."

The Lord is calling to me—getting closer, closer. But I cannot answer.

She heard no more... until she opened her eyes and saw herself being pulled out of the hole.

Suzanne had no feeling, it was like a dream. *It doesn't hurt at all.*

She was safe now. She could close her eyes again.

"Oh, my darling, my precious darling. You're nearly frozen to death!"

Leif? Leif, are you in heaven, too?

Chapter Eleven

When Suzanne opened her eyes, she was not in heaven, but was tucked in a sleeping bag in the front seat of Adam's vehicle. The heater was on and she was getting warm.

"No, no. Don't try to sit up," Leif cautioned comfortingly. "You're safe with me now. Just stay curled up next to me as I drive. You need to conserve your strength and your body heat. We'll be at the Woloskis' within five minutes. "Then will be time enough to find out what was going on and to call the sheriff. I got the pickup's license number as it sped away."

"He . . . he wants to kill me! Is Mr. McArthur following us? Watch out, he'll try to ram us over the cliff!"

"You *knew* the man. . . ?"

Frightened, Suzanne bolted upright and twisted to look out the back window. They were driving through the middle of Hastings and no one was behind them. She turned and looked at Leif.

"You're not the Lord," she said, surprised and shivering.

Leif's laugh was one of relief. His eyes twinkled. "Nor are you a drowned kitten, but right now you look like one."

She quickly examined herself in the visor mirror. Her hair, damp and matted, framed a washed-out complexion. Her lips had a slight blue cast. She folded back the visor and looked down at her clothes.

"I look as if I've used up several of nine lives. Are you sure that you don't want to throw me back in that hole and see if you can pull out something better?"

Even as the words came out of her mouth, she was sorry she'd spoken them. He'd saved her from that madman McArthur or from a freezing death. Never in her lifetime would her narrow escape be a joking matter.

"And bring about my own demise? Matt would . . ."

"Matt? What's he got to do with this?"

Leif stopped in front of Ned and Bessie's. He opened his door and got out. He turned and looked at Suzanne. His eyes had lost their sparkle.

"Matt flew with me this morning, remember? He told me then how much he loves you. It seems to be no secret that he's hoping the two of you will marry before he moves to his new pastoral post next spring." Leif shut the door and walked around the vehicle.

Suzanne was astonished! Matt had not asked her to marry him, although it wouldn't surprise her. What did surprise her was Matt's pending transfer—he hadn't mentioned a word.

Suzanne opened her door from the inside. Before she could climb out of the sleeping bag, Leif scooped her up, bag and all, and carried her to the front door. Bessie responded to the doorbell. "Ned, come quick. Something's happened to Suzanne!" she called out in the direction of the kitchen as Leif placed Suzanne on the sofa in front of the fireplace and tenderly propped pillows behind her head. He took away the half wet, emergency sleeping bag that Adam always carried in his truck, and replaced it with a hand-knitted wool afghan that Bessie handed him.

Ned limped into the room on his cane and took a chair near the sofa. "It's getting to be a habit—using our sofa as a portable nursing home," he mused. "What happened to you this time? This fellow get you stuck in the snow while trying to beat the preacher's time?"

"Ned, you keep still!" Bessie ordered as her eyes scowled their own warning at the erring husband.

Suzanne was aware of Leif's eyes on her—awaiting her reaction. She chose to ignore Ned's remark.

Leif spoke up. "Matt almost lost his bride this morning, but not to me, unfortunately. Some drunken fool was stalking her with a rifle in the field near the airport during the heavy snow flurry we had earlier."

"He'd have hit me with his first bullet if it hadn't been for the protection of those beautiful snowflakes!"

Ned leaned forward on his cane. The fire crackled in the background. "You're serious? First the fire in the church, now someone actually tried to gun you down? I know what you're saying is true. It's just unbelievable that anyone would want to harm . . ."

"I don't know who set fire to the church. But the man who rammed my car, attempting to send it out of control and over the cliff, and who chased me with a rifle in a snowstorm, was Holly's father!"

Ned jumped from his chair. His face was rage-red. He threw his cane into the far corner and shouted. "I knew McArthur was a crackpot! You live around kids as long as I have and you get a sixth sense about some things."

"What made you suspect him, Ned? He's never around school."

"He doesn't have to be. When a child's personality changes drastically in a short period of time, as Holly's has, it's time to find out why. Almost always, the trouble is in the home. Generally, too, the culprit is the father."

"How...how do you know that?" Suzanne asked.

"Either he hasn't got his household in order, allowing injustice of some nature to prevail, or he's the festering sore himself. The result is the same. The abused child, backed into a corner, has nowhere to go but within."

"Oh, Ned, I'm her teacher. I should have seen..."

"Maybe not. She works hard at making it appear everything is fine. The last thing she wants to do is to attract attention. It didn't all come together in my own mind until during that night after the fire. "I woke up in a cold sweat, suddenly knowing, as sure as I'm standing here, that Holly didn't forget that money in her desk—she'd stolen it. My guess is she'd mouse-holed it a little at a time from motel receipts. Her desk was her own personal refuge in the world, a safe hiding place—until she could gather enough courage, and what she felt was enough money, to run away."

Suzanne thought back to the surprised look on McArthur's face when she handed him the sack of money. She cringed at the memory of his display of anger as he drove off.

"And I exposed her plan when I gave Mr. McArthur her cache! Oh, what have I brought on that child?" Suzanne buried her head in her hands.

"Is that what caused him to flip out and come after you this morning, Suzanne?" Leif asked. He was trying to tie the pieces of the puzzle together along with the rest of them.

Suzanne recounted, for Leif's benefit, Holly's slip in the snow, Holly's pain when she'd put her arm around the girl's waist and of the 13-year-old's disappearance from the sofa she herself was now lying on.

"I drove out to the motel this morning, determined to speak with Holly, privately. Her parents told me she was with Mrs. McArthur's sister for the weekend."

"Not true," interrupted Ned. "Mrs. McArthur has no sister. 'No relatives' it says on Holly's student application."

"That's whose folder you took!"

"Right. I took it down to the courthouse and checked on a few other facts."

"What did you learn, Ned?"

"That McArthur has a criminal record. The sheriff helped me with that part. The family moves frequently. They've been here about as long as anywhere."

"Why have they moved so often?" asked Leif.

"Sheriff Blake told me, after he made a few private calls, that the McArthurs move when the school or neighbors start making complaints about possible child abuse. They move out of that county, overnight sometimes, to avoid investigation."

"Attempted murder is a charge he can't outrun," stated Leif. "But we still don't understand how you ended up in that lonely field, darling."

Suzanne felt the color rise to her cheeks. *A pet name for Jessica, no doubt.*

Suzanne tried to take her mind off Leif's slip-of-the-tongue by launching into a detailed description of her flight for life once she'd threatened to involve the sheriff.

"We must find Holly now!" she concluded. "Holly might really be at the motel. If so, he's holding her captive!"

Suzanne panicked at the scene her frayed emotions drew in her mind. Mixed into the picture of Holly bound and tied, hurt and abused, was the scene, long-repressed in her own mind, of the night she was dragged into a darkened room by a wayfarer her father had taken in.

Engraved in her brain forever were the horrible words he used as he tried to rip her clothing from her. She'd fought him with every ounce of strength. Her muffled screams finally alerted her younger brother. The man bolted past the investigating youngster and was out of the house and into the woods before her father, called from the shower, was able to reach her side.

Suddenly, all the ugliness in that wayfarer, in Holly's father, mingled together, trapping her in an icy coffin in an isolated snowfield. A tear trickled down her cheek, followed by another and another. *Dear Lord, protect Holly from that wicked, wicked man. Help us to find her—soon!*

Leif came to her and gathered her into his arms. "It's all right to cry, my darling." Suzanne did not push him away. Instead, she put her head on his shoulder and began to sob. Years of pent up anger, terrifying fear, and childhood embarrassment flowed away in cleansing tears.

Finally, she raised her head. Leif's eyes were wet, too. She accepted a box of tissues from Bessie and said, while wiping the tears from her long lashes, "After I heard Mr. McArthur's third shot, I felt myself losing control of my senses. I thought I'd died and gone to heaven."

"Third shot? McArthur fired only two," Leif stated. "The third shot was mine, fired from the rifle Adam had mounted on his window gun rack. I fired it at McArthur's feet to scare him off. It did the trick. I got his license number as he drove away, then I followed your tracks in the snow until I found you."

"Tracks in the snow!" Suzanne gasped. "He could have..."

"Yes," Leif nodded. "He could have done the same thing—and found you without firing a shot. But because he did fire that first shot, I stopped working on Adam's plane in the hangar and rushed outside in time to see a recognizable splotch of yellow plowed into a snowbank down the road. I was outside to hear McArthur's blood-curdling threats ring out across the field."

Suzanne felt faint. "God was in control all the time," she whispered through fresh tears that fell silently down her cheeks.

Ned hobbled to the front door and grabbed his coat off the peg. "Come on, Stevens. Let's get the sheriff and get out to that motel."

"I'm with you. Let's call Sheriff Blake first, and set up a meeting place this side of the motel. It will save time."

Ned nodded agreeably. "He may want to bring help."

"God be with you all," prayed Bessie.

"Amen," whispered Leif.

"Meanwhile," said Bessie, "I'm taking this girl upstairs and slipping her into a hot tub."

Suzanne allowed Bessie to pull her up from the sofa and to lead her up the stairs. She had no idea how exhausted she felt until that moment.

The two reached the landing in front of the guest room. "You go on in the bathroom and start getting off those damp clothes. I'll get your robe from the guest room."

Suzanne nodded wearily.

A moment later, she heard Bessie on the landing, excitedly calling down to the men as they were going out the front door.

"Forget the sheriff. Call Doc Shaw. The child, Holly, is asleep on Suzanne's bed!"

Chapter Twelve

The aroma of Bessie's freshly-baked pump-kin pies floated lightly into the living room where Suzanne kept a solitary, Sunday after-noon vigil in front of a lazy fire. Ned had gone to the airport with Leif and several of the other men following an early prayer service Matt conducted especially for those involved in the search.

Suzanne heard Matt's footsteps on the land-ing. He descended the staircase and walked across the room, dropping down on the sofa beside her, saying, "That's powerful medication Doctor Shaw prescribed. Holly's headed for Dreamland again."

"Did you two have a good visit?" Suzanne asked softly.

"Yes," he nodded thoughtfully, staring into the fire. "Counseling is one of my favorite aspects of the ministry, but this situation is tough—I think my father, at his age and with his experience, would find it no less heartbreaking."

Suzanne thought of the years she'd carried the burden of just one brief, attempted "incident." Her heart ached for Holly, who had endured a whole childhood of abuse. Then, a few weeks ago, her father demanded that Holly "make herself available" to certain motel guests. Holly's mother sided with her husband, against her daughter, insisting that everyone in the family must do what was necessary to make the motel a success. Holly had been beaten when she continued to refuse.

It will take more than heavy sedation to put Holly back together again. Lord, You know Holly's spiritual, physical, and emotional needs. Guide us each in the direction of Your will. Help us make Holly whole in every way.

Finally, Suzanne spoke aloud. "I heard that the sheriff and his men had no trouble apprehending the McArthurs last night. He was passed out drunk on the bed and she was well on her way toward the same state of oblivion when the two squad cars arrived."

"The McArthurs knew their time clock was about to run out. They had to realize that after that final, horrible beating McArthur gave Holly over the stolen money. Her escape was nothing less than a miracle."

Suzanne squirmed uneasily at Matt's reminder. "Three cracked ribs and a hopscotch pattern of ugly bruises on her body. What do you think will happen next, Matt?"

"Her parents will be arraigned in court tomorrow on child abuse charges. You've already given your statement to the sheriff. The district attorney will handle the attempted murder charge separately, I think. He'll be calling you."

"What will Holly have to go through?" asked Suzanne.

"The case worker, who was out here last evening to interview Holly, will speak for her in court tomorrow. Holly will not have to attend this time. Doctor Shaw and I will also testify tomorrow morning. We hope that Holly will not be sent to a juvenile hall facility or to a foster home—but without respectable relatives. . ."

"Could. . .could we keep her?" asked Bessie from the kitchen door.

"Bessie, what a wonderful idea!" Suzanne exclaimed. "Is it possible, Matt? It would be a wonderful solution."

Matt got up and walked over to Bessie and put his arm around her shoulders. "Are you sure? Wouldn't you like to think about it, talk it over with Ned, first?"

Bessie shook her head. "No. Ned and I already talked it over early this morning before church. He's going to ask Adam to speak to Judge Churchill tomorrow on our behalf."

"Bessie, you and Ned are..."

Bessie interrupted. "We'd better not count on it before it happens. The disappointment would be... well, let's just say, we've had that guest room fixed up for several years for a foster daughter. We just never got up enough courage to ask the welfare department to start their investigation of us. When Ned's arthritis started bothering him seriously, he decided we were too old."

"What changed your minds?" asked Suzanne.

"Having you here for the weekend, Suzanne—and all the commotion it's brought into this house, including that poor waif upstairs. It used to be like this when our Camille was alive. She died in her sixteenth summer—a freak diving accident at a church outing at Sweetwater Pond on the Stevens Ranch."

Oh, Ned. No wonder you didn't want to talk about the Stevens Family. We all seem to have pockets of pain in our lives that take a long, long time to heal.

Bessie was saying, "We'd forgotten how much we missed being involved with the young."

"You got more than you bargained for when you got me," remarked Suzanne, with a wisp of a warm smile.

"It's been our blessing. Ned and I dreaded the thought of you returning to your rooming house tonight. We intended to ask you to move here permanently—until we found Holly in bed upstairs. We think she needs us as much as we need her."

"You have me to speak for you also tomorrow, Bessie," Matt said, giving Bessie a lingering hug.

Just then the telephone rang. Bessie stepped into the kitchen to answer it. "It's search headquarters. Caroline Wilder for you, Suzanne."

Suzanne took the receiver from Bessie, who returned to the kitchen to check on her baking.

Suzanne listened and responded, "That is odd. What did you tell her? Another call? Who gave them the headquarters number? Never mind, I think I know. I'll be right over."

Suzanne put down the phone and turned to Matt. "Jessica's taken matters into her own hands. Three clairvoyants have called Adam's Rib in the past hour with 'private' information concerning the crash. Caroline asked me to come over and discuss it with her. I don't know what good I can do..."

"Maybe she just needs company. Caroline's been manning the radio most of the day. She's also trying to get ready for Monday morning's breakfast crowd."

Suzanne laughed lightly. "This was the weekend they were supposed to be closed as I remember. They've been busier than ever."

Matt handed Suzanne her coat. "Come on, I'll drive you over. If you get out today a little, going back to school tomorrow won't be such a shock," he teased.

"All right, so I wasn't at church this morning. It's my first miss since I moved to Hastings. Anyway, Holly, Bessie, and I had our own mini-service at the same time you were having your church service."

"What text did you choose?"

"Bessie selected Psalm 121 for our meditation. We concentrated on the first two verses: 'I will lift up mine eyes unto the hills, from whence cometh my help. My help cometh from the Lord, which made heaven and earth.' I believe I was comforted as much as Holly was by those precious words."

"And you didn't have to stand up or carry cold, summer lawn chairs into the bare-walled building," he teased.

"Well, wherever two or three are gathered..." she teased back.

"That reminds me. Martha Pettijohn suggested to me after church that perhaps the reason you didn't attend today was because you were afraid the person who set fire to the church was still out to get you."

"Oh, really! Her question answers two questions."

"How do you figure?" Matt asked.

"First, news of what happened yesterday at the airport hasn't reached her ears yet. That means the link in her gossip chain wasn't involved in any way in 'the event.' By the time we ended last evening with the sheriff's team, the doctor, Leif and his crew, Adam, his wife, other searchers and all of us in this house—a lot of people had been informed, but not Martha."

"I don't get the point you're trying to make."

"Repeat what Martha said to you on the church steps this morning."

"She said, 'Is Miss Flynn afraid that the person who set fire to the church is still after her.'"

"Matt, how many people know that the gas lines had been tampered with—that the fire had been deliberately set?"

"You...and I...Bessie and Ned, and evidently Martha Pettijohn."

"Which means..." prodded Suzanne.

"Which means she's the firebug or knows who is!"

"Now what do we do, Matt?"

"We continue to keep still. Our tactic has served us well so far. It's narrowed the field considerably."

Just then, Bessie came back into the room. Matt advised her in a soft tone, "When Holly wakens, share your invitation with her. The judge will want to know how she feels about it."

"What if she doesn't want. . ."

"Bessie," he said reassuringly, "this is the home she came to when she needed love more than anything else in the world."

Suzanne felt her eyes begin to glisten. *Oh, Matt, you are a special person—truly a man of God. You deserve a wife who appreciates and loves you dearly. I appreciate you, I. . .*

"Are you coming?" Matt was holding the front door open for her.

"Oh. . .yes," she smiled.

Chapter Thirteen

Suzanne hurried down the front steps. Matt closed the Woloskis' front door. She looked up and was surprised to see Jake McCafferty coming up the walk toward them. His attention was focused on Matt.

"Pastor, Mr. Georges took sick while we were up searching. I brought him down right away and took him home. Doctor Shaw is with him now."

"What's the matter with him, any idea?"

Jake stuffed his hands in his pockets and looked at the ground. "He's dying. I discovered that the first morning we went up together. Same symptoms my sister had. When I asked him what ailed him, he rolled off a complicated medical term. He didn't think I'd know what it meant. I pretended I didn't.''

That's why he stopped complaining about Mr. Georges' company and his trip to the faith healer. He has a compassionate corner in his heart after all.

"Has he asked to see me?" Matt inquired.

"I told him I was coming to get you, but. . .it's me who really needs to talk with you."

"I'll walk on to the restaurant," Suzanne said.

"No, stay. I just want to ask a question. What do you think of Mr. Georges' faith healing?"

Finally, Suzanne thought to herself.

"It's not what I say, it's what the Bible says. The inspired Word of God should be our only guide," replied the young minister.

"Then give it to me. What's it say about this kind of healing?"

Matt smiled. "I wouldn't dare tell God whom or how to heal. There are numerous miracle healings in the Bible. We also know that the devil has the power to cure. It's not an easy subject. First John 4:1 says, 'Beloved, do not believe every spirit, but test the spirits to see whether they are from God.' If we truly want to know the truth and are willing to be obedient to His Word, God will help us to discern between good and evil."

Jake sighed. "That's about the same thing Mr. Georges told me. I guess I should have talked to you before spreading gossip. I'd like you to go back to Mr. Georges with me. I've got to do the right thing and own up to being the one who knifed him in the back. I owe him that."

"Sure," Matt said, "let's go now. Come on, Suzanne, we'll drop you by on the way."

A few minutes later Suzanne was at Caroline's side. She'd just hung up the phone.

"That's another one—the fifth. I found out that Jessica paid three of them $500 each to 'take the case,' with a promise of doubling it when the plane is found. The others are offering their services free, in hope of being rewarded when their prognostications are declared correct."

"Three of them? If they disagree, which two are phonies? Imagine, the other two are the 'ambulance chasers' of the psychic world." Suzanne shook her head and continued, "I foresee chaos."

"Right. Listen to this. One of the paid psychics says there is no life at the crash site. The other two say there is. One says the plane is at the bottom of a ravine; another insists it hit a tree at the 7,000-foot level, near an abandoned cabin. The third paid seer declares the plane landed in a clearing and is covered with snow. What happens if all of them are partially correct?"

"I don't see that the search team has been helped by Jessica's un-Christian approach at all," sighed Suzanne.

"Wait until word of the $5000 reward gets around."

Suzanne gasped and spun around at the sound of Leif's voice. "What $5000 reward?"

"The $5000 reward that Bill Daniels' company put up this morning. I found out about it a few minutes ago when I called Len. News of the reward has already hit the national wire services, according to him."

The phone rang, again. Caroline walked over to pick it up. While she was occupied, Leif said in a confidential tone, "I discovered that Daniels' business partners aren't coming up to help search because they're too busy fighting over Daniels' job. Everyone wants to be president."

Then the two heard Caroline say, "No, I am not authorized to accept a collect call. If the party wishes to leave a return number..." Evidently, the party didn't. He had hung up.

Leif looked directly at Suzanne and said, "It was getting too overcast to see the ground so we called it a day. I borrowed Adam's Suburban so that I could take you for a ride." Then glancing at Caroline, he asked, "Do you mind if I whisk Suzanne away for awhile?"

The phone rang one more time. "No, go ahead. It looks like I'll be too busy to visit anyway." She waved them a quick good-bye and turned to answer the telephone.

Leif took Suzanne by the arm and guided her quickly toward the front door. He pulled both their jackets from the coatrack and kept going until they were safety outside, beyond a telephone summons.

He helped Suzanne into her fur-trimmed parka and hurried her to his side of the vehicle, parked only a few steps across the parking lot. He opened the door and gave her a boost.

"Scoot over as fast as you can. This is a fire drill," he ordered teasingly.

"What's the hurry?" she asked as he drove hurriedly out of the restaurant parking area, turned sharply into the street, and headed out of town.

"I can't believe we've done it!" he exclaimed excitedly, rolling down the window halfway, letting the cold mountain air wash over them.

"Done what?" she asked, feeling a sense of freedom as the wind blew through her long hair and brushed a pink flush over her cheeks.

"Gotten away from the rest of the world and the pressure of the search for just a little while."

"Pressure—I've not known you without a burden on your heart. From the moment we met, the top priority in your mind has been organizing your uncle's rescue. He was still on your mind when you stopped everything and saved my life."

"I've been generously rewarded."

"Oh?"

"I got to hold you while you dissolved into a bucket of tears. You're here beside me now, when not long ago you told me that you didn't want to be my friend."

"What kind of man are you when you're not under pressure, Leif Stevens?"

"I don't know, really. I've discovered I have two lives. My life, prior to this week, was filled with designing orbiting space stations, serving on the building committee of my church, playing on a church basketball league and on a company soccer team, and dealing with my changing goals in my relationship with Jessica."

I thought we were getting away from the world for awhile. I guess Jessica is part of his world, wherever he is.

"I apologize for my unkind remark concerning Jessica's efforts to help in the search. I'm certain I do not fully appreciate the frustration she's going through having you so preoccupied. I'm sure she feels helpless."

Leif laughed, then glanced at Suzanne.

"One thing Jessica's not is helpless—headstrong, maybe. We don't need that kind of help on the search. Jessica knew my feeling —I was adamant in the matter of clairvoyants in our private conversation before breakfast."

"Your relationship, your pending marriage with Jessica is not my business, but is she a Christian?"

"No."

Suzanne opened her mouth to ask a question, then thought better of it. She turned her head and watched the enchanting winter scenery drift by.

"The answer to the question you're not asking is, when Jessica and I were first engaged it was all right with me that we have our own spiritual beliefs. That's a very personal matter. It was enough, we each thought at the time, that we shared the chemistry of love, the spark that made secular activities fun, worth sharing.

"As I got deeper into the Word in our men's Bible study, I began to feel uncomfortable with our arrangement. I saw that God has a definite plan for the family, beginning with the husband, who must have his house in order."

" 'As for me and my house, we will serve the Lord,' Joshua 24:15, another wonderful memory passage," commented Suzanne. "Our study was in the New Testament, Ephesians 5:21-27, where Paul clearly states the importance of Christ as the cornerstone of marriage. Jessica and I were starting off on the wrong foot."

"What did you do about it?"

"I went from telling myself that she'd become a Christian once we were married, to asking her to join a Bible study with me now, before marriage."

"And..."

"She hangs on to her humanism more adamantly, the dearer my Christian faith becomes to me. Finally, last week, she gave me back her engagement ring."

That's why she wasn't wearing one when I picked her up at the airport. I should have sensed something then.

Suzanne showed her puzzlement when she asked, "But you introduced her to me as your fianceé."

Leif sighed. "An effort to keep a mission project alive, I guess. The hiring of the psychics drew the final battleline. Her feeling is that if it's so important to be united in a faith, it might as well be hers, as followers of 'The Church of Humanistic Love.' To assent to the hiring of clairvoyants—wouldn't I employ *any method* to find my uncle?—would suggest that Christ isn't the only way to salvation."

"You seem to be at an impasse."

"No. It's over. She was at Len's when I called him for his report. She and I talked...until there was no more to be said between us. I'm frustrated that I could not bring her to faith, but I am at peace that we are no longer considering marriage to one another."

"Faith is not ours to give. Only God gives faith. All we can do is share what Christ means to us, personally," remarked Suzanne.

Sometime during their discussion Leif had rolled up the window and it was beginning to get cozily warm in the cab. Suzanne sensed then that the tingling excitement she felt racing through her veins had not as much to do with the exhilarating cold air as with Leif's company.

"You said that you had two lives. What's the other?"

"I'm basically a happy, optimistic person. Although my mother refuses to talk about Hastings or our life here, I have only fond memories of my early childhood on the ranch. However, each time I mentioned my interest in returning here for a visit, my mother forbade it. By the time I was old enough to make my own decisions, I was involved in getting an education or getting a job. Other interests were in the forefront of my life."

Leif paused, as if reflecting. "Strangely, my uncle invited me to come up here fishing with him last summer. When I told him that I was too busy, that I'd like a rain check, he said, 'Don't fight your destiny much longer, boy. You're missing the best life has to offer.' "

"Is your uncle a Christian?"

"Oh, yes. He was a wonderful inspiration to me. He took my father's place, which was difficult to do. I owed him a great deal."

"You're using the past tense..."

Leif reached over and took her hand. As he wound his fingers through hers, she noticed that his dark eyes deepened. She placed her other hand on top of his, giving him all the support she could.

"I am, aren't I? I've come to accept that the reason we haven't found Bill Daniels' plane is not because it isn't in our search area, but because the plane iced-up, spun out of control into a nose dive and crashed, breaking into a million pieces on impact. We haven't found the plane because there's not a piece of metal large enough to spot from the air."

"Oh, Leif! What a horrible, frightening picture..." There was nothing she could think of to say to assuage the grief she knew must be twisting through his heart. All she could do was to be there next to him...as a friend.

Leif slowed the vehicle and turned onto a half-hidden lane that meandered up through a forest of snow-dipped pines. A blue-tailed bird fluttered above as if welcoming the visitors into a fairyland bordered by an icicle-spangled fence line. Handfuls of diamond sparkles, broadcast over the snowy meadows, caught the darting sunlight and danced for the awed pair as they drove up the mountain. A squirrel ran up a tree and disappeared into a dark hole. A jackrabbit bounded into the road and raced ahead of the Suburban at his own staccato rhythm until he alone decided to leave the road as quickly as he'd entered it.

"What a beautiful winter setting. I've never been up this road before. Where does it lead?" She prayed that her interest would lift his spirits.

"This, dear Suzanne, is the entrance to the Stevens Ranch. Just over the top of this hill should be the ranch house, if I remember correctly."

A minute later they crested the ridge and there below them spread a panorama of beauty that escaped comparison. In the center of the scene was a rambling ranch house. To one side sat a two-story barn, corrals, and beyond stretched field after field. A windsock frame in the lower foreground marked the site of a long runway.

"Leif, it's beautiful! May we drive down to the ranch house?"

"No, not this trip. You see, the road isn't cleared. I don't remember exactly where it is. I know there's a creek and a bridge somewhere between here and there. It's too risky. I don't want to chance getting Adam's vehicle stuck. We're a little too far out to call for help."

"I thought you had a caretaker out here?"

"We do. His cabin is in those trees to the left, see?"

As Suzanne looked Leif's way, he put his arm gently around her shoulder. It felt wonderful.

She began to tremble.

"I'm sorry, you must be getting cold," he said, removing his arm and flipping on the heater switch. "It's also getting late. I'd better get you back before I have Matt to answer to."

Matt! I haven't thought of him this whole trip. Nor have I ever answered Leif's question regarding a wedding date...Matt told him that he was hoping to marry me before...I've not told either one of them...

"A dime for your thoughts. I'm willing to pay the price of inflation," Leif said, backing the four-wheeler around and heading out the way they came in.

"I was just thinking how tempting ranch life must be to the man who has found unexpected comfort in Levis and a lambskin jacket."

"That does fit well with the 'second' me. Look," he said, pointing out the front windshield. "What's that coming down the snow-covered slope about a half-mile south?" Leif pointed to a small figure traversing its way to the highway.

"We'll get a closer view once we're on the main road. It looks like someone on snow-shoes."

Both were quiet as Leif made his way care-fully back to the main highway. Suzanne con-centrated on keeping the growing figure in sight, lest it disappear into a ravine and they lose sight of it.

Leif reached the main road and, after one more longing backward look, turned toward town. They reached the figure about a mile down the road.

"It's an Indian girl, Leif. She's taking her snowshoes off and putting them in the straps on her back. She evidently plans to walk toward town."

"Let's give her a ride. She still has miles to walk. What could be so important as to send her on a long journey on a Sunday after-noon?"

As they pulled closer, Suzanne exclaimed, "It's Morning Flower. She's about Holly's age. She lives on the reservation up in those hills that overlook the eastern high desert."

"How do you know her? Does she come in-to school?"

"No. They have a teacher on the reservation. A missionary brings them into the church youth activities once in awhile."

Leif pulled to a stop. The girl looked fright-ened until she caught a glimpse of Suzanne.

Once she was tucked into the cab between them, Suzanne asked, "Why are you walking to town, Morning Flower? It must be very important."

"The rancher who brought the message to my people said that it is very important. My brother found some things. I'm bringing them to town to show the man who is looking for the airplane."

Leif pulled over and stopped. "I am that man. What do you have to show me?"

Morning Flower pulled out a kerchief. She untied it and handed Leif three objects the size of the palm of his hand—three pieces of charred airplane metal.

Chapter Fourteen

"Everyone's signed Holly's get-well card, Miss Flynn," said the class president, handing Suzanne a large, blue, construction-paper piece of art.

Suzanne smiled, holding the card up for all to see. "It turned out beautifully, didn't it? The hospitality committee is to be congratulated for such a clever design, as well as each of you, for your contributions of original poems and personal comments of encouragement."

Suzanne lovingly tucked the card into a

file folder, saying, "I'll deliver it to Holly right after school. I know that she will look forward to thanking each of you personally in three or four days—as soon as Doctor Shaw says she may return to school."

Just then, the final bell rang and the room became a mass of movement in all directions as a symphony of noise filled the air. During the next three minutes desks popped up, slammed down, books opened and banged shut, chairs squeaked, coats rustled, boots tromped, metal lunch boxes clanged, and adolescent voices twittered the scale from soprano to bass.

Finally, the last straggler, dragging her coat tie on the ground behind her, closed the classroom door. It was suddenly quiet.

Suzanne was glad the day was over and that the class had readily accepted her explanation that Holly had met with an unfortunate accident, suffering cracked ribs and bruises. She also told them that Holly was staying in town, at the Woloskis', near the doctor's, for the time being.

Suzanne carefully stacked papers to be graded—a project for another afternoon. Right now, she was anxious to get over to the Woloskis' to check on Holly and to deliver Holly's card from the class. Typical of the age, the young teen was obsessed with concern over what her classmates thought of her absence.

Suzanne pulled off her eel-skin high heels and put them into the cupboard and took out her fur-lined boots. She brushed the chalk dust from her forest-green, wool tweed suit and fluffed the soft ruffles of the rose-red blouse that brought out the soft pink of her high cheekbones. While putting on her parka, the young teacher picked up her purse and that special file folder. Then she closed and locked the classroom door and hurried down the arcade.

She enjoyed walking. It was her best thinking time. But today, all day long, during math, science, geography, English—her mind had been preoccupied with questions that could only be answered at the end of this longest day of her life.

What happened in court this morning? Did the judge allow Holly to remain with Bessie and Ned? If so, for how long? Was Mr. McArthur released after the arraignment? Is he free to chase me down again in a vendetta for his arrest? She shivered at the possibility.

Overriding her concern for Holly and herself was the question that had her insides tied up in knots. *Were the charred pieces of airplane metal part of Bill Daniels' plane?*

Rancher Johnson, Morning Flower, and Leif left at dawn that day to travel the sometimes impassable roads onto the Indian reservation. They hoped to locate Morning Flower's brother, who had picked up the foreign objects, from among thousands scattered over a quarter mile area on the high desert floor. According to Morning Flower, her brother came upon the devastation while herding cattle. When he returned to the settlement, he was told of Rancher Johnson's visit and of the search underway for the crashed plane. Due to Johnson's stressed urgency, the condition of the family truck, and the unpredictability of the roads, it was decided to send Morning Flower overland to Hastings.

Suzanne calculated that the group could have possibly reached the supposed crash site by noon. Depending on what they found, the earliest that they could return to Hastings would be nightfall.

Although her mind swam with questions, it was Suzanne's heart that ruled her feelings. Tears welled up and spilled down her cheeks as she sensed the anguish Leif must have felt as he approached the crash site.

She could only imagine the soul-deep pain that coursed through his body as he identified the twisted wreckage as belonging to his uncle's flight—or of the blessed relief that was his if it were not.

Blinking back the free-flowing tears as she walked, Suzanne chided herself.

Leif should not have hiked into that area alone without a friend. I should have been at

*his side. . . I wanted to be at his side. He was
there when I needed him. I let him down the
first chance I had to repay his friendship. Why
didn't I call in a substitute for today?*

Suzanne hurried the last few steps to the
Woloskis', dabbing the tears from her cheeks.
She ran up the steps, two at a time and burst
through the front door. She would not wait
a minute longer; she would call the Johnson
Ranch for the latest news!

"Miss Flynn! Miss Flynn!" Holly exclaimed
the second she saw Suzanne come through the
front door. "I get to stay here until the end
of the semester!"

"The judge will review the situation at that
time. There's a possibility Holly will be staying until the end of the school year. . ." added
Ned, before Bessie could interrupt. The three
converged upon Suzanne excitedly.

"We've applied to be a foster home. Perhaps
Holly will be able to stay permanently, if
things don't work out for her at home," Bessie
managed to interject.

"Wait, wait," Suzanne's tear-stained face
broke into a smile that matched each of theirs.
"I can't absorb all this good news at once."

Then Holly said, "What did the kids at
school say about me today?"

"Oh, I almost forgot in all this excitement,"
Suzanne replied, pulling the festive card from
the file folder. "Here. The entire class sends
its love and prayers. They know you've had

an accident but expect you to be back in time to participate in the spelling bee on Friday."

Holly took the card eagerly. Her eyes sparkled with adolescent freshness, long overdue in her life. She turned away and walked to the corner chair, where by the winter light, she devoured privately the hand-written messages of encouragement. Suzanne knew by Holly's enraptured expression that a national treasure couldn't have meant more than the understanding of her peers.

Suzanne glanced at Ned and Bessie. Both beamed contentedly as they quietly sat watching the rebirth of self-esteem in their new "daughter." Ned wasn't retiring next month—he and Bessie were beginning a new adventure in living!

Suzanne heard a soft rap on the door. The Woloskis seemed not to notice, so she tiptoed over to answer it. It was Matt.

"I didn't want to waken Holly with the door bell," he whispered. Suzanne placed a finger to her pursed lips, then she gently backed Matt out the front door and closed it behind them.

"Holly's doing much better and the three of them don't need us right now," Suzanne confided in a pleased tone. Then she asked, "How did things go in court this morning?"

Matt nodded toward his car and started

156 • FOREVER YOURS

down the steps. She followed. Matt didn't answer until both were settled in the car and he'd started the engine.

"Fine," he said, backing out of the drive and heading north. "McArthur was held without bail. He was sent to the county jail to await arraignment on several other charges, including attempted murder. Bail was set for Holly's mother. She was returned to the women's detention facility until someone bails her out."

"Oh, Matt. How terrible for Holly. Does she know?"

"Oh, yes. She knows. Holly didn't respond one way or another when the caseworker told her. Later, the caseworker told me that Holly's reaction was not unusual, under the circumstances—sort of a protective insulation against an emotional breakdown. A child psychologist will be seeing Holly at least twice a week for some time to come. Meanwhile, the caseworker suggested that the best place for Holly is in school, surrounded by caring friends."

"And we are that," sighed Suzanne.

Suddenly, Suzanne stiffened as the word "friend" flashed in front of her mind's eye. "Stop the car, Matt. I don't even know where we're going, but I've got to get back to Woloskis—now!"

He slowed to make a U-turn. "What did you forget?"

"I forgot to make a telephone call. I want to call the Johnson Ranch. Mr. Johnson and Leif must have reached the crash site by now and radioed the results back to the ranch." Suzanne knew her voice sounded high-pitched, nervous. She couldn't help it. She was desperate to share Leif's feelings, whatever they were.

Matt sped up again, his hands wrapped tightly around the wheel. "You can use the phone at Mr. Georges'. It's closer to go there now than back to Ned's."

"Is that where we were going anyway?"

"No. I had another spot in mind, down the road. However, I don't think you're going to be very receptive to anything I have in mind until you have peace in yours."

Suzanne's imagination raced.

We were headed for Lookout Point, I'm sure of it. He probably wanted to tell me about his upcoming transfer. Perhaps... perhaps he was going to ask me to come with him—as his wife. Suzanne could feel her pulse quicken. The moment of decision was nearing. She knew it.

"What were you saying, Matt? I'm sorry, my mind wandered for a moment..."

"No apology needed. I know your thoughts are back on that high desert, Suzanne." Matt reached over and took her hand. "It's been an intense week for all of us. We're all anxious for the search to end. I promised to look in on Mr. Georges this evening sometime. We might as well double-duty it and stop by first. He'll be anxious to know the results of your call, too."

Mr. Georges' redwood cabin was modestly quaint. A blazing fire in the natural stone fireplace kept the one-bedroom home warm and cozy. And as Matt thought, Mr. Georges was eager to hear the latest news on the search. He excused his nurse to take a few minutes off and run an errand. He would get in his visit with Minister Matt while Suzanne called the Johnsons.

Suzanne found the ranch number listed in Mr. Georges' dog-eared church directory that was hanging on a string next to the kitchen wall phone. While she waited for an answer, Suzanne glanced around the old bachelor's kitchen. There wasn't a modern appliance in sight. *It's as if Mr. Georges lives in the past.* She noticed that religious books were piled on top of the refrigerator, the kitchen counter, and on the breakfast table. Suzanne hadn't realized Mr. Georges was such a student of the Bible.

The phone rang several times at the other end. She'd let it ring a few more.

Suzanne picked up an old, 1929 World's Fair medallion lying on the counter. While she was looking at it, the coin slipped from her fingers, dropped to the floor, and rolled toward the back porch.

Finally, discouraged, Suzanne hung up the phone. She started toward the living room where Mr. Georges, propped up in his rocking chair, was listening while Matt read to him from the New Testament.

Suddenly, she remembered the coin that had rolled into the back porch. She turned and followed its path into the darkened room. She moved her foot around in an arc but failed to locate it.

Next she fumbled for the light switch. No switch. She waved her hand overhead, hoping to bump into a string hanging from the ceiling. A second later, the string was in her hand. She pulled it and the tiny room lit up. There, in the corner was the elusive coin. Suzanne dropped down to retrieve it. It had come to rest under the old-fashioned coatrack by the back door. She scooted forward, picked up the medallion, and brushed it off.

What this house needs is a thorough housecleaning, she said to herself, rising up and brushing against the rickety coatrack. She reached out to steady the tittering antique when she saw it.

Suzanne gasped. The blood rushed from her head. She was so stunned she could hardly move. Then the adrenalin started to surge through her veins. She became enraged.

Suzanne pulled the light string, returning the room to darkness. She strode into the kitchen, tossed the telltale coin on the counter, and marched into the living room. She crossed the room purposefully and stood above Mr. Georges.

Anger flashed in her eyes and in her voice.

"Mr. Georges, why did you set fire to the church?"

Chapter Fifteen

"Suzanne! What are you saying? Mr. Georges saved your life. Besides, he's ill..."

"Dying is a more appropriate word, my boy," interjected the old man, holding up a shaking hand to silence Matt.

"Matt, I know he..."

"Stop it, both of you," Mr. Georges ordered with a cranky voice. "The false accusations of the past couple of months have shortened my life. No matter, I have only days left now—and I don't intend to fill them with bickering."

Matt was on his knees in front of the frail figure. "It's unbelievable! You wouldn't have set fire..."

The old man's voice toughened. "Why not? What's unbelievable is that we would allow the house of God to become a money changers' paradise one weekend a year!"

"Wha...what do you mean?" Matt's voice was almost lost to him in his state of shock.

"I voted against the annual desecration of our church by that blamed Harvest Blessings—throwing muslin over the lecturn, pushing the pews back. It's a wonder the church council didn't vote dancing in the aisles!"

Suzanne blinked her eyes. Was she really witnessing...

"We have no business buying and selling in the church! Each year, I've gained additional support for my position—until this year. Those wicked false rumors have completely destroyed my credibility."

Matt took the old man's hands into his own.

"Dear Brother, Christ was not angry because there was buying and selling in the temple. The merchants were selling doves and other sacrifices God demanded to the pilgrims who had traveled far. What angered Christ was the downright thievery of the money changers, the price-gouging of the merchants, the disruption of the worshipers."

"I had no time left to regroup..."

"Dear Brother," Matt began patiently again, "I do not agree with the Harvest Blessings Festival either, but for a different reason. I feel that each of us should give to the work of the Lord, freely, without expecting something in return—be it a pie, a homemade quilt, or a used book. Not only do we compete with Adam's Rib when we serve supper, we take profit from our local merchants by spending our hard-earned money at the bazaar. The thousands of hours spent each year in making the craft items, baking, and collecting saleable goods for the festival could be spent in Bible study and evangelism. We are the only church within miles. There are so many unchurched..."

As Matt counseled at the feet of the dying man, the fire burned low, silhouetting Matt and Mr. Georges against the waning winter's daylight. A lump rose in Suzanne's throat and strangled the rage in her heart.

She stepped into the background and took a seat quietly by the fire, continuing to watch the tender scene between the patient man of God and the erring child of God.

The old man nodded, signifying understanding as Matt continued softly, "Each of us has the right to hold to our opinion—both are motivated by a desire to strengthen the body of Christ on earth. But that motivation is not a privilege to believe that the end justifies any means."

"I've got to confess," sighed Mr. Georges weakly. "I was moved some by revenge. Gossippers destroyed my last chance to win votes for forgetting the festival. They should suffer, not me."

Matt lowered his head. An anguished moan rose from deep within him.

Suzanne wanted to go to him, comfort him, but she could not. The Master Comforter Himself was ministering to him now. She sensed His closeness more than ever before.

"I never intended to hurt Suzanne. I ran into her by accident. I'm not too steady on my feet these days. . ."

"I know that," Suzanne whispered from the edge of the flickering light.

"The fire exploded around me. I didn't expect that. I hurried back to the vestibule as soon as my own head cleared, and tried to pull her out. It helped to have Ned come along. He'd heard the bell toll."

Suzanne rose and tiptoed toward the two men. She dropped down and knelt beside Matt. She laid her hand on Mr. Georges' arm and looked up into his tired, fading eyes.

"I forgive you," she said clearly.

Mr. Georges whispered hoarsely in return, "May God forgive me, too."

Chapter Sixteen

"Come, sit closer to me, my dear Suzanne," Matt said, pulling her into the circle of his arm.

The twilight was "turning on the stars," as she remembered telling her father when she was a little girl. She felt much like that little girl now, overwhelmed by all that had happened in her life during the past week, and unsure if she was ready to venture forth into the next day.

"Relax, it's all over now," Matt said softly. "It's been a long time since you and I could just 'be' together." He pointed to the distant rock formation across the canyon from Lookout Point. "Watch how the blue turns to purple, then to black as night folds upon us."

It was no use. Although she'd set aside the sight of the seered jacket hanging from the coatrack in Mr. Georges' back porch, she could not forget the sound of the unanswered telephone bell at the Johnson Ranch. She had tried once more, just fifteen minutes ago, before leaving Mr. Georges' house.

"I'm sorry, Matt. It has been a long day, a long week."

"Do we have a little time before this day ends to spend a few more moments together?" he asked, a touch of hurt entwined in his words.

"Of course," she smiled. "I was just feeling a little sorry for 'poor me.' "

Matt smiled. She could see his eyes begin to dance in the ebbing light.

"I have some special news to share with you."

"Oh...?" she questioned, raising her eyebrows. She felt her pulse quicken.

"The church council president sent me a letter. I'm to be transferred to another church after Easter."

Though he tried to hide it, Suzanne noted an edge of enthusiasm in his voice.

"How exciting! A new challenge!" she

responded warmly. "Congratulations, I'm very happy for you, personally—very sad for the void you'll leave behind in Hastings."

"How does Suzanne Flynn, woman, feel about Matt Owens, man, leaving the area?"

Suzanne tensed at Matt's bold directness. She moved uneasily in place to bide for time. Then, perturbed with herself, she turned and faced Matt. "You are my dearest friend. I will miss you desperately," she replied sincerely.

"I love you, Suzanne. You know that I do."

"Yes, Matt, I do," she whispered, allowing him to move her again into the circle of his arm. "And I love you..." Her thought was unfinished. They both knew it.

"This is the most difficult moment in my life, my dear Suzanne. I...my heart wants to reach out and beg you to marry me—soon. I need you at my side when I move on to the unknown..."

Suzanne pondered. A week ago she would have been tempted to say, "Then what's keeping you? Ask me." Now, unlike that night on the moon-drenched veranda, she did not need the advice of the pounding cadence surging through her body. In her heart of hearts Suzanne knew she could not marry Matt.

"...But my head warns me that it would be a mistake for both of us," Matt announced reluctantly.

Suzanne was thrown off balance. "Why?" she asked innocently.

"Because I want the woman I marry to look at me...the way you look at Leif. I need her to be so anxious about my well-being that she can hardly contain herself until we are together..."

Suzanne felt her face turn crimson in the darkness. She lowered her eyes.

Matt put his hand under her chin and raised it. She opened her eyes and looked at him. He was smiling.

"I want, I need, a Christian wife who is more than my best friend."

"You deserve much more, Matt."

"We both do. Christians, above others, have the example of Christ's love as a guide in choosing a life partner. God Himself created the chemistry of love that attracts one to another. It would be a sin to ignore the importance of that mutual spark of love."

"I want the same in a marriage, Matt."

"I know that. You'll have all of it with Leif," he said kindly.

Suzanne sputtered, "He's never said a word ...you imagine...I don't believe..."

"Stop, my dear Suzanne. I apologize. I'm guilty of fishing. My comments are premature."

Then, before Suzanne could comment again, Matt said, "Before we close the subject, I want you to know that I look upon our extraordinary and special friendship as part of God's plan. He has shown me the standard I may expect in the wife He is preparing for me. That's exciting to me, Suzanne."

"Oh, Matt." Suzanne, overcome by his words, threw her arms around Matt's neck and began to cry. "You honor me more than I deserve. It's a privilege to be called your friend."

"Then let's quit while we're both feeling good about ourselves—and before you get an ulcer worrying about Leif." He gave her a quick kiss on the nose, then dabbed her tears with his handkerchief. A moment later, he was backing away from Lookout Point.

During the ride into town, Suzanne and Matt chatted comfortably. They talked once more of Mr. Georges and the fire. "How do you suppose Martha Pettijohn knew that the fire had been deliberately set?" Suzanne asked.

"I don't think she really knew. It wouldn't take long for the question of arson in one person's mind to mushroom into fact on the gossip chain. Had we not known the truth, her comment Sunday in front of church would have slipped by me unnoticed."

"What happens next regarding Mr. Georges?"

"As soon as we get back to town, in about 30 seconds, I'll call an emergency meeting of the Board of Elders. I have no other choice."

Matt turned onto Main Street. "I'll drop you here at Adam's Rib. All right? It would be Leif's first stop."

Suzanne nodded nervously in agreement as Matt turned into the restaurant parking lot. She spotted Adam's Surburban parked near the entrance. Suzanne opened her door before Matt slowed to a stop. As soon as he did, she hopped out.

"If Adam's there, ask him to meet me at the parsonage in 30 minutes, okay?"

"Okay," she called back over her shoulder. Suzanne was already at the front door.

Once inside, Suzanne quickly scanned the room for a sign of Leif. He was not in the room anywhere, nor was his jacket hanging on the rack by the door.

Just then, a hand touched her elbow as a voice spoke softly behind her ear. "He's in my office waiting for you."

Suzanne turned and looked into Adam's sober brown eyes. He didn't have to say anything. She knew the words he was unable to utter.

"Matt . . . Matt wants to see you at the parsonage within the half hour. Board of Elders meeting . . . it's very important."

"It must be. I'll go now. You get on into my office." Adam gave her a quick hug, turned away, and strode out the door.

Suzanne looked fearfully at Adam's office door for just a moment before she hurried toward it.

She knocked softly, then entered without

waiting for a reply.

Leif bolted from the leather couch and came toward Suzanne with his arms outstretched. His eyes were bloodshot, his face drawn, tired looking. To Suzanne, he was still incredibly handsome.

She walked into his arms and they closed around her. He stroked her long hair as if he were comforting a little girl. Leif didn't speak for what seemed to Suzanne a very long time. When he finally did, his voice was hoarse.

"It was their plane."

Those few words, spoken simply, sent the sensation of hot lead racing to the pit of her stomach. She clung frantically to Leif, for fear that the heaviness would melt her into the floor. Her ears were suddenly filled with the dizzying sound of a single-engine plane crying out helplessly only a few feet above her in a treacherous blizzard.

They had been so close—to death.

Suzanne slumped. Leif scooped her up and carried her to the couch. He set her down gently and poured her a glass of water from the pitcher on the end table, holding it for her while she drank. Then he took both of her small hands into his and held them tightly.

"We arrived at the spot mid-morning. It took only minutes to determine what had happened. There was no definite point of impact. The wreckage was scattered as far as a quarter of a mile in one direction from the main area of debris. I believe the plane iced up, spiraled down, and broke up before it hit the ground."

"Oh, Leif!" Suzanne buried her head in her hands. Leif immediately pulled her close to him once again.

He continued, still holding Suzanne close. "Johnson called his base unit on the radio. The operator called the authorities and the FAA investigators were at the scene by mid-afternoon. They helicoptered in from Reno. They have already removed what remains could be gathered into plastic sacks..."

Suzanne stiffened.

"Oh, my darling, I'm sorry. I shouldn't..."

"No. It's better that you talk it out. Besides, we both know that your uncle is not in those ...he's long gone. He is home in heaven. We rejoice in that fact—and in that he did not suffer. It is only those who still live who suffer the loss."

"What you say is so true. I spoke those same words to my aunt only a few minutes before you arrived. Still, I need to hear them for myself."

"Friends," she smiled, "are for comforting."

Leif looked thoughtfully into her eyes for a long time. Suzanne felt that familiar tingle wash over her. She lowered her eyes quickly and asked, "What are your plans now?"

"Oh...yes. Plans. Adam will drive me into Reno in the early morning, where I will catch a plane to San Francisco. I will visit my aunt and Mrs. Daniels and make the burial arrangements. Then I will drop by my office and see if I still have a job left."

Suzanne was speechless. It suddenly hit her that Leif *did* have another life—hundreds of miles away. Jessica was out of his life—but so was she!

"What's the matter? You're suddenly white as a . . ."

"It's nothing," Suzanne insisted, rubbing her fingertips against her right temple. "The shock of your uncle's death . . . the concussion . . . I think they're working together to confuse me." She tried to smile.

Leif started to say something, but Suzanne stopped him when she spoke first. "It's time for me to say good night. School days begin early in Hastings and I'm sure that you have other calls to make before you call it a day." She got up from the couch.

Leif pulled her back down beside him. "I'm not as easily dismissed as your students, Suzanne. I have more to say. And the evening is still young."

Suzanne gulped. She'd never seen this man with the glint of fire in his eyes. She wasn't quite sure what to expect next. She settled back. Leif's eyes softened immediately.

"I would like to have a memorial service for my uncle here in Hastings next Saturday. Adam has promised to arrange it with Matt. Would you help Adam notify all who helped in any way at all with the search, especially those on the prayer chain whom I've never met?"

"Of course, I'll take that responsibility. It won't take long to get the word out." *Thank You, Lord. I will see him one more time.*

"And will you be sure that Morning Flower and her family are there? I'd like to present the reward money to them after the service."

She nodded.

"You asked about my plans. It occurred to me this evening that I am now the sole owner of the Stevens Ranch. It will be quicker, easier than I expected, to meld my two lives into one. By the time the spring thaw sets in, I will have cleared up my affairs in the city and be on my way, moving van and all, to Hastings. My goal is to return the Stevens Ranch to a full, working ranch and its ranch house to the magnificence of its early days. I will also have the room I need to restore old airplanes and fly . . ."

"Leif, I am delighted beyond words!"

"If I hurry, I figure that I can make it back up here before you and Matt marry and move . . ."

"Before Matt and I? Matt is leaving after Easter. I am not going anywhere."

"You're not? That's wonderful! I . . ."

He didn't finish. He pulled her tightly to him, then lowered his lips to meet hers. He kissed her tenderly at first, then drew back and looked at her lovingly. His eyes sought hers and read the desire of her heart. Once again his lips found hers. This time, Suzanne's head spun madly as he kissed her longingly, hungrily.

"You've turned the saddest day of my life into my happiest," he whispered. Then he kissed her again.

Chapter Seventeen

The next four days passed in a daze, yet at the same time Suzanne could recall each word of Leif's nightly telephone calls to her.

"This telephone courtship is ridiculous," he said on Tuesday night. "I'll be glad when I can court you properly. Does Hastings have a movie theater?"

Suzanne laughed. "No, but we have high school basketball games in the gym on Friday nights." They talked for two more hours, reveling in their time together.

On Wednesday night, Suzanne told Leif the

story of the fire in the church, from beginning to end, filling in the parts he didn't already know. "What did the Board of Elders finally decide to do?" he asked.

"The church is 'self-insured' so no investigation is necessary. The chairman of the board called on Mr. Georges. The man is at death's door and repentant. As Adam said, 'The church looks better now than before the fire. It needed repair and painting. It did us all good to pitch in and get it done in a hurry.' "

"That's Adam," Leif chuckled. "Always a positive thinker. How about the stained-glass windows and the pews?"

"Well, that is another matter. The stained-glass windows are too expensive to replace. The holes will stay boarded up until spring when the trustees will decide what to do. As for the pews, the Board decided that we'll continue to bring our own chairs for awhile. No one is anxious to dip into the social hall building fund to buy pews. Besides, new ones wouldn't fit the decor of a 100-year-old church."

"We've been on the phone an hour," Leif noted. "I can't imagine the two of us ever running out of things to talk about. I know that I will never tire of saying, 'I love you.' "

Suzanne smiled to herself and replied, "That's the first time you've told me."

"I promise that it won't be the last."

Later that evening, after she'd said her

evening prayers, Suzanne lay in the darkness of her room, looking out at the moon-bathed sky. "A lovers' moon" her mother would have called it. "It stirs up the passions of love. And love is often fickle," her mother warned.

Suzanne fell asleep wondering if a stray moonbeam had magically touched Leif in San Francisco.

Thursday evening Leif began with, "I have a surprise for you."

"May I guess?"

"Of course, because you'll never get it."

"Is it bigger than . . ."

"Yes," Leif laughed. His voice rippled across the phone line, sending a wave of joy through Suzanne. "Yes, it's bigger than a bread box. Can you be more imaginative in your speculation?"

"No, but I can counter with a surprise of my own. And I'm willing to give you a clue. It's a gift of love from more than one of us."

The line was quiet for a moment, then Leif said, seriously, "All I need is your love, Suzanne."

Suzanne glanced out at the moon. It was hidden behind a cloud. The magic spell was broken and still he loved her. "I love you, too, Leif," she replied from the bottom of her heart.

Suzanne fell asleep that night counting

the hours until Saturday morning.

•　•　•

Suzanne awakened early on that special morning. It was too quiet. She threw back the covers, dashed to the window, and pulled back the heavy drape. It was snowing! For the first time since she'd moved to the High Sierra she was disappointed to see snowflakes falling. It meant that Leif and Len could not fly into Hastings in time for breakfast as planned. Instead, they would have to fly a commercial airline into Reno later in the morning, rent a car and drive up, reaching Hastings barely in time for the services. She found that she did not have time to sulk over the change in Leif's schedule. There was too much to be done. It began with Matt's visit while she was finishing a piece of toast.

"I dropped by to see if your eighth-grade choir is ready for their first performance. I'm printing up the bulletin this morning. I can put it in or leave it out, as you please," Matt said, half teasing.

"Matt Owens, don't you dare leave them out! Caroline and her sewing crew have the new choir robes finished and pressed. I admit, we weren't planning to perform before Christmas Eve, but I think you'll be pleased. Holly is directing. She has a natural ability for it."

"What really pleases me, Suzanne, is the

spirit of love that prevails among our members. It's a transformation that began when they were called together for the search and to refurbish the church. Each had to stop and give of himself *then*. They were tasks that money couldn't buy. It took every person we had, working in harmony. The reward, Mr. Dunlap told me, was 'the good feeling of giving.' "

"The rate of gossip has slowed down, according to Caroline. The women so enjoyed putting on the potluck at Adam's Rib the first day of the search that they insisted on repeating it today after the service," Suzanne said, handing Matt a piece of freshly-buttered toast.

He took it, saying, "New friendships have been formed through all of this, and none more intriguing than the McCafferty-Georges combination. Which reminds me of the most exciting news of the day. Jake McCafferty is opening his home for a men's cottage Bible study on Tuesday evenings."

"Praise God!" Suzanne exclaimed.

Matt beamed. "You've got that right. In fact, that's my sermonette title for the praise service today. Note, a praise service, not a funeral service. Praise God, our brother has been called home to heaven. Let us rejoice."

"I think I'm getting the sermonette right now," Suzanne giggled. She glanced at her watch. "It's time for me to get to choir practice. Are the evergreens hung in the church and the advent wreath in place?"

"Of course. Adam and I did most of that last night. It smells like Christmas in the sanctuary. The high-schoolers hauled in benches from the gym and all the extra banquet chairs from Adam's Rib. No one has to bring his own seat, today only...and maybe Christmas."

Matt walked to the front door. "I've got your coat. Let's go. I'll walk you to church. It's time to turn on the new heater and get the place warmed up. Two o'clock is not far off."

The morning sped past in the bustle of excitement of families driving in from distant ranches, bringing food for the potluck and in time to visit with friends without the pressure of the search shrouding them.

Fortunately, the previous night's heavy snowfall had laid a thick coat of white over the mud and slush that had been Hastings' bane for the last few days. The town presented its pristine best as Leif and his best friend drove up in front of the church at 1:45, just the moment Suzanne stepped out of the vestibule and onto the steps.

In keeping with Matt's spirit of joy, Suzanne had chosen to wear a smartly-styled white wool suit set off with black accessories and a high-collared black silk blouse. She also wore a perky black hat. The red stripes in the hatband picked up the red in the pin on her lapel. Suzanne's makeup was subdued but flatteringly youthful.

Leif stepped from the car and started up the steps, never taking his eyes from Suzanne. He smiled approvingly at her appearance. Suzanne smiled back at the handsome man wearing a black wool suit, white shirt, set off with a black tie with a dignified red design, and completed with a white handkerchief in his breast pocket.

Just as he reached her, the muffled church bell began to toll softly. He took her gloved hand into his and following her nod, turned toward the street.

People climbed out of warmed cars parked along the street and in the parking lot. Others, opening their umbrellas against the light snow beginning to fall, walked silently across the block from Adam's Rib. Leif and Suzanne stood motionless, greeters on the church steps, watching as Hastings' residents answered the bell's tolling to come and pay last respects to one of their own.

Adam and Caroline were the first to ascend the steps and shake Leif's hand. "Welcome home, my boy" were his only words. No more needed to be said. Caroline and Suzanne nodded to one another in understanding.

Leif welcomed and called by name all those he'd met during the grueling days of the search. Others arrived and greeted Leif whom he had not met—members of the prayer chain, telephone tree, fuel brigade, radio relay, and shuttle bus teams. Suzanne stood beside the man she loved and introduced each of those people to Leif as they stepped up. He repeated each person's name, shook hands, and expressed to each his sincere appreciation on behalf of his family and himself. Suzanne marveled at Leif's composure under the circumstances.

The bell stopped tolling. It was 2 o'clock. The church was overflowing. Organ strains of the beautiful advent hymn of praise, "Lift Up Your Heads, Ye Mighty Gates," floated out the open doorway. Suzanne turned toward the church door.

"Wait," Leif whispered, slipping his arm through hers. "Before we go into church and walk down that center aisle together, I want you to promise me something."

"What... what do you want me to promise?" she asked, looking up into his adoring eyes and wondering what could be so urgent as to make them late into church.

"I want you to promise me, my darling... the next time we go down that center aisle together, it will be as my bride."

"Oh, yes, my love. Now I am the happiest woman in the world. I am forever yours!" She moved quickly, joyfully into his waiting arms.

He kissed her eagerly, pressing her tightly against him. Suzanne's head spun as her body seemed to melt into his.

The organ strains grew louder. Suzanne drew back, a warm blush on her cheeks. Leif bent and kissed her once again. He sighed deeply, squeezed her hand, and then turned with her and walked into the crowded vestibule of the church. The worshipers parted silently as the couple made its way down the center aisle. Leif and Suzanne took their places in the front row as the music ended.

As Matt delivered his well-prepared message, Suzanne allowed her eyes to scan the room. She noticed many worshipers who'd slipped past them at the front door. She nudged Leif. To the far left was Morning Flower, the girl who had trudged miles in snowshoes to bring Leif his long-awaited news. To Suzanne's knowledge, Morning Flower still didn't know of the $5000 reward that was her family's. The money could mean a newer truck or a college trust fund.

In the row behind the Indian family was Carlton Wickland, who only a few of the searchers knew about. He'd donated most of the fuel for the Hastings search planes. He'd given the reason for his unsolicited donation to Adam as, "I knew Stevens when he ranched these parts. We were fishing buddies."

Leif, overwhelmed by the outpouring of love represented, bowed his head and drew out his handkerchief.

Lord, I know that You sent Matt here to prepare our hearts. You sent Leif's uncle to

evangelize to this community, and Leif so that
we could demonstrate Your message of love
and salvation. Keep us ever mindful of this
lesson, that we may build, not backwash, in
generations to come.

Then she heard her precious choir begin to
sing. She took Leif's hand and squeezed it.
"This is our gift of love to you," Suzanne
whispered softly.

From the balcony came the precious Christmas words, "Let us all with gladsome voice
praise the God of heaven, who to bid our
hearts rejoice, His own Son hath given. To this
vale of tears He comes, here to serve in
sadness, that with Him in Heav'n's fair homes
we may reign in gladness."

"In death, the message of life through Christ
...thank you, Suzanne, for that love message," Leif whispered.

As the choir hummed the last verse, Matt
raised his arms and gave the blessing. Then
he took a step toward the congregation, surprising Suzanne by saying, "I would like to
conclude this service of praise with two exciting announcements."

Everyone was silent. "First, two gifts have
been presented to Hastings Community
Church in memory of Carl Stevens' homecoming, by the Stevens Family and a sister
congregation in the faith in San Francisco.
That church is tearing down an older, small
chapel to make way for a larger, modern

house of worship. Together, they are supplying us with pews enough to fill our church and stained-glass windows in the number we need to repair our church."

The gasp in unison was followed by only a second of silence before applause filled the old church. Suzanne looked up at her beloved with tears in her eyes. He smiled knowingly down at her, slipped his arm around her, and handed her his handkerchief.

Matt raised his hand. When the room quieted, he smiled and said, "There's more. The best is still to come."

A wave of chuckles spread through the room. "I am assured that these improvements will be completed in time for our Easter celebration." A general murmur of approval filled the room.

"Secondly," Matt said, dabbing his own eyes, "it gives me great personal pleasure to announce that on the Sunday following Easter, which will be my last Sunday among you, I will have the privilege of uniting in marriage at this altar, Mr. Leif Stevens and Miss Suzanne Flynn."

Suddenly, the church bell rang out. The organist began the triumphant recessional. The congregation stood—and waited. Matt, smiling, nodded to Leif.

Leif took Suzanne's arm in his and escorted his happy, misty-eyed bride-to-be down the center aisle and out of the church.

Dear Reader:

We would appreciate hearing from you regarding the Rhapsody Romance series. It will enable us to continue to give you the best in inspirational romance fiction.

Mail to: Rhapsody Romance Editors

Harvest House Publishers, 1075 Arrowsmith, Eugene, OR 97402

1. What most influenced you to purchase **FOREVER YOURS**?

   ☐ The Christian Story   ☐ Recommendations
   ☐ Cover   ☐ Other Rhapsody
   ☐ Backcover copy   Romances you've read
   ☐ _____

2. Your overall rating of this book:
   ☐ Excellent   ☐ Very good   ☐ Good   ☐ Fair   ☐ Poor

3. Which elements did you find most appealing in this book?
   ☐ Heroine   ☐ Story line
   ☐ Hero   ☐ Love Scenes
   ☐ Setting   ☐ Christian message

4. How many Rhapsody Romances have you read all together?
   (Choose one)   ☐ 1-2   ☐ 3-6   ☐ 7-10   ☐ Over 11

5. How likely would you be to purchase other Rhapsody Romances?
   ☐ Very likely   ☐ Not very likely
   ☐ Somewhat likely   ☐ Not at all

6. Please check the box next to your age group.
   ☐ Under 18   ☐ 25-34   ☐ 50-54
   ☐ 18-24   ☐ 35-39   ☐ Over 55

Name _____

Address _____

City _____ State _____ Zip _____

Rhapsody Romances

- ☐ **Another Love**, Joan Winmill Brown — 3906
- ☐ **The Candy Shoppe**, Dorothy Abel — 3884
- ☐ **The Heart That Lingers**, June Masters Bacher — 3981
- ☐ **Love's Tender Voyage**, Joan Winmill Brown — 3957
- ☐ **Promise Me Forever**, Colette Collins — 3973
- ☐ **The Whisper of Love**, Dorothy Abel — 3965
- ☐ **If Love Be Ours**, Joan Winmill Brown — 4139
- ☐ **One True Love**, Arlene Cook — 4163
- ☐ **Reflection of Love**, Susan Feldhake — 4201
- ☐ **Until Then**, Dorothy Abel — 4171
- ☐ **Until There Was You**, June Masters Bacher — 4198
- ☐ **With All My Heart**, June Masters Bacher — 4104
- ☐ **Forever Yours**, Arlene Cook — 4383
- ☐ **Let Me Love Again**, Joan Winmill Brown — 4392
- ☐ **My Heart To Give**, Carmen Leigh — 4368
- ☐ **The Tender Melody**, Dorothy Abel — 4287
- ☐ **Touched By Diamonds**, Colette Collins — 4279
- ☐ **When Love Shines Through**, June Masters Bacher — 4309

$2.95 each

At your local bookstore or use this handy coupon for ordering.

HARVEST HOUSE PUBLISHERS

1075 ARRROWSMITH, EUGENE, OREGON 97402

Please send me the book(s) I have checked above. I am enclosing $_____ (please add 50¢ per copy to cover postage and handling). Send check or money order—no cash or C.O.Ds. Please allow four weeks for delivery.

Name _____

Address _____

City _____ State _____ Zip _____

Phone _____